P9-EMK-375

F·C
GEE

DATE DUE

The
CHAMPION

The
CHAMPION
Maurice Gee

Simon & Schuster Books for Young Readers
Published by Simon & Schuster
New York   London   Toronto   Sydney   Tokyo   Singapore

Blairsville High School Library

SIMON & SCHUSTER BOOKS FOR YOUNG READERS
Simon & Schuster Building, Rockefeller Center
1230 Avenue of the Americas, New York, New York 10020
Copyright © 1989 by Maurice Gee
Originally published in New Zealand in 1989 by Penguin Books
Limited. First US. edition 1993. All rights reserved including the
right of reproduction in whole or in part in any form. SIMON & SCHUSTER
BOOKS FOR YOUNG READERS is a trademark of Simon & Schuster.
The text for this book is set in Garamond #3.
Manufactured in the United States of America.
10 9 8 7 6 5 4 3 2

Library of Congress Cataloging-in-Publication Data
Gee, Maurice. The champion / by Maurice Gee.
        p.   cm. Summary: In 1943 twelve-year-old Rex sees his quiet
New Zealand village dramatically changed by the arrival of a black
American soldier on leave from the war. 1. World War, 1939–1945 —
New Zealand—Juvenile fiction. [1. World War, 1939–1945 — New
Zealand—Fiction.   2. New Zealand—Fiction.   3. Afro-
Americans—Fiction.   4. Race relations—Fiction.] I. Title.
PZ7.G2578Ch 1993 [Fic]—dc20   92-37670 CIP
ISBN: 0-671-86561-7

Contents

The
CHAMPION

1

Shooting Hitler

What do you answer when people ask "Who was the most important person you've ever known?" They don't mean *important* in the way a politician is said to be, or a football player or film star or rock singer. They usually mean someone not well known, someone who made you see things in a different way.

It's a hard question. Most people, in the end, answer "Mom and Dad," or "my big brother," "my big sister," "Auntie Joyce," "Uncle Dick." And I can make that sort of answer too. Mom and Dad—my poetry writing mom, who never stopped hoping, who never stopped trying to make other people happy, and gabby tricky Dad, my crooked dad—helped make me what I am, no doubt about it. And my sister Gloria played her part, and so did

Grandma and Grandpa in their crazy way. But I can give another answer too, name the one who came and went and left me a different person. It was Jackson Coop. He changed my life—Jackson and the things that happened in those two weeks in February 1943.

I was twelve. I'll try to speak with my sixth-grade voice, not my grown-up voice. I want to say how it was and not change the shape of it by putting in ideas I've thought of since. So I have to time travel, go back in time, put myself in those days, say, "This is it."

Well, this is it, a place to start from: the house in Barrington Road, Kettle Creek, New Zealand. The kitchen had paneled walls and brown linoleum curling at the edges like stale bread, and a black wood-burning stove in an alcove with a wire drying rack above. Hanging there were steaming socks, navy-blue girl's rompers, barber's aprons dried as stiff as boards. (Mom was often late with the washing.) The living room had a red-brick fireplace and books on the mantelpiece—poetry and novels and a book called *The Maori Race,* which I thought was about running. A rose in a stained-glass window gave a lovely sunset glow to light from the porch. We had three bedrooms, mine a narrow one with two narrow beds. The bath in the bathroom stood on iron legs like tiger claws. The enamel was worn through, with black iron patches where you sat. If you knelt and looked underneath you could see pieces of dried-out soap against the wall and cigarette butts Dad had dunked in the water and dropped down there when he soaked in the bath reading his racing form. The broom wouldn't reach that far, Mom said.

There was no hot water, not till after the war. When we wanted a bath we boiled water in a big copper kettle and carried dangerous buckets from the washhouse—where the wringer was clamped on the wooden tubs, where empty coal sacks thrown in the corner bred spiders that I believed were poisonous katipos, where Dad's padlocked cupboard stood upright and secret behind the door.

The house was a bungalow needing paint. It stood on a quarter-acre section with undug garden, unclipped hedge, and scraggy lawns. Dad wasn't any good with lawnmower and spade. He said, "A barber's got to keep his hands in good shape." So does a pool player.

On the morning of the day Jackson arrived, I was out on the back lawn in my pajamas shooting Hitler and Tojo with my BB gun. Hitler you've heard of. Tojo was the Japanese war leader. I drew him with slanty eyes, forty-five degrees, and buck teeth coming to his chin. Hitler had a blacked-in forelock hiding his left eye and a mustache like a Maori bug. (This is my sixth-grade voice. *Maori bug* isn't used today.) I had stuck the drawing on the open end of a cardboard box so I could get my BBs back. You couldn't buy BBs during the war. Standing on the back gravel driveway I shot Hitler and Tojo from a distance of twenty feet until only tatters of them were left. "Take that, Hitler"—dead center in the mustache. "Take that, Tojo"—in the spectacles. I feared them but I had the upper hand. Sniper in a tree, behind a wall, I won the war with a single shot, time after time.

We played games of that sort in the war years, stalking Germans in the grass, bayonetting Japs—and dogfighting in Spitfires, arms straight out, making a high-pitched drone on the roof of our mouths and going *rat-tat-tat* with our tongues. Down went the Messerschmitts and Zeros in flames. "Take that, Jerry!" "Die, yellow dog!"

The Japanese had us scared for a while. They came down the Pacific so fast, taking Singapore, which wasn't an American but a British place, taking the islands one by one, and sinking the *Repulse* and the *Prince of Wales*. We had air-raid drills at school. The siren blew in town and we filed out of our classes into trenches dug in the acacia grove. We put up blackout curtains and watched the sky for bombers and the sea for periscopes. But now, 1943, the danger was over. Tojo was stopped at Guadalcanal. He wasn't going to get to New Zealand; he wasn't even getting to Australia. We liked the Yanks and cheered for them in the pictures and still ran out to see jeeps driving through Kettle Creek; but we turned our interest back to the real war, where our men were, the one against Hitler.

So there I was on that morning, shooting Hitler twice to Tojo's once, when Mom put her head out the kitchen window and said "Rex!" very sharply. I was so deep in my game it was like being slapped, which was more than she'd meant. Mom couldn't be cruel if she tried.

"Mom," I cried, "you made me miss. Now I've lost that BB."

"Never mind the BBs," Mom said. "You get the milk pail down to the road or there'll be no milk for breakfast."

"I can't go in my pajamas."

Gloria stuck her head out beside Mom's. She was wearing curlers in her hair, two in front, two at the sides, and little tin things like spring clips here and there. "He's scared Dawn Stewart will see him," she grinned.

"Why can't Gloria do it?"

"It's not my job." She disappeared.

Dad came out the back door. Dad was something of a dandy in the shop. Sometimes he wore a bow tie—he wore it for billiards—but at home he liked to be comfortable and went around in shirts with their collars off and baggy old trousers held up with old suspenders. He was heading for the outhouse up behind the hedge to read his racing form.

"Come on, Daniel Boone, get a move on." My BB gun made him choose Daniel Boone. If I'd been on my bike he'd have called me Destry or Tom Mix and if I'd been in a tree it would have been Tarzan. These out-of-date heroes made me cross. I'd settle for Bill Ross of the Lost Commandos if I had to, but the one I most wanted to be was Rockfist Rogan of the RAF.

"Daniel Boone," I said disgustedly. I went to my bedroom and pulled on my clothes, reading my *Champion* at the same time. This was a boys' weekly magazine that came from England and sold for fourpence. (That was about ten cents in American money, I learned later.) It had stories about Rockfist and Bill Ross and Colwyn Dane the detective and Fireworks Flynn and his soccer team, the Freebooters, and Gusty Gale, the junior captain at Greystone School. These last two I hardly bothered with. I read Rockfist three times before I turned to them. I was in the middle of a story about Rockfist luring the Hun ace into a fight by pretending his Spitfire was crippled when Mom came in and pushed the milk pail at me and whipped away my *Champion* with her other hand.

"She's nearly at the gate."

"I've got to get my shirt on," I complained.

"You'll do it faster if you don't read. And," she said, going out, "get that stuff cleared off the bed. Someone's got to sleep in it tonight."

"Who—" I started to say, but she was gone. Sometimes Mom could be like a whirlwind. Her dreaminess was annoying but I liked it better than her bouts of mad activity that left you dizzy and not knowing where you were.

I ran down the walk with the pail, wondering who was coming tonight. People were always sharing my room, friends of Dad's from Auckland mostly, caught in Kettle Creek for the night. (That meant they'd played cards too late to catch the bus.) I hated them because they came to cook up deals with Dad, and some of them looked young enough to be away fighting in the war, so why weren't they? And some kept me awake by snoring all night. Mom gave me pieces of rags to stuff in my ears but that made them ache.

She was right about nearly missing the milk. Mrs. Stewart's old Dodge truck with the special low bed was only two houses up the street. She was ladling milk into a pail that Dawn, her granddaughter, held up. I'll have to tell you more about these people fairly soon, because they're a part of those two weeks, Jackson's story, a very big part. But for now I'll just say that Mrs. Stewart owned a farm, a crummy sort of farm, on the edge of town, by the mangrove swamps, and our half of Kettle Creek bought its milk from her. Dawn lived with her—just the two of them. Dawn was in my class at school. Mrs. Stewart was white and Dawn was half Maori.

She put the full milk pail on a gatepost, then grabbed our next-door neighbor's and came for mine. On the way she passed our garage where Dad's car, the hearse, poked its hood over the sidewalk. It was too long for the garage and Dad always parked it with its rear doors inside, "for very good reasons" he said with a wink. That meant things he had to leave inside, hidden under sacks. Don't be alarmed. It wasn't bodies—he was a barber not an undertaker and he had the hearse only because he hoped to get an extra ration of gasoline (he never did). As she passed, Dawn slowed down and ran her hand along the grille.

"Hey," I shouted, "keep away from that."

"Who wants your stupid car?" She snatched my pail and ran to the truck, which had moved down the street. Mrs. Stewart climbed on the back and ladled milk from the urn to the pail. Dawn looked up and seemed to ask a question and Mrs. Stewart waved her away. You could hardly tell if Mrs. Stewart was a woman or a man, in her plaid shirt and overalls and her hair as short as mine. There was a muscular stringiness in her neck and a bony hardness in her hands. She jumped down from the truck just like a man.

Dawn put our neighbor's pail in its box and gave me ours.

"Hey," I protested, looking inside.

"It's not my fault."

Mrs. Stewart was getting in the cab. "Mrs. Stewart, we get more than this."

"We're short today," she said indifferently, and drove twenty yards down the street.

"You're cheats, Stewart," I said to Dawn.

"We are not."

"We're not paying for a full one."

"Who cares?" She ran for the next milk pail in her clean sandals and skirt. I was in bare feet, with buttons off my shirt. Mom had got out a needle and thread last night to sew them on but had put them down somewhere and couldn't find them. I didn't like Dawn's clothes being better than mine.

I went up the walk with the milk and put it on the back step while I chose clods of earth from the dried-out flower-bed by the kitchen window and lobbed them at the Hitler/Tojo box. They burst on contact, which was satisfying, but I didn't score any direct hits. The outhouse made an easier target. I chose a clod the size of a grenade and pulled the pin out with my teeth and overarmed it high over the clothesline, over the willow hedge, dead center onto the iron roof, where it exploded, raining bits of dirt everywhere.

"What the hell!" Dad yelled.

"Direct hit," I said, and escaped inside with the milk pail. I put it on the bench in the kitchen, where Gloria was making her school lunch, and got my *Champion* from the bedroom and sat down. I straightened my spoon at the side of my plate. Mom just plonked stuff on the table but I liked things four square. I was, I'd heard her say, "an elbows-in-at-sides sort of boy." She was at the stove stirring bread and milk in the porridge pot. The radio was playing "Chattanooga Choo-Choo," one of the tunes of that year.

"There's no more lemon honey," Gloria yelled.

"There's Marmite in the cupboard." Marmite is some brown, bitter stuff you spread on bread. It's supposed to be good for you. Mom carried the pot to the table and dumped mounds of bread and milk in our plates. I didn't complain. What was the use? I hated bread and milk but left-over bread had to be used.

Gloria brought the milk from the kitchen. "Old Ma Stewart gave us short." She poked the bread and milk. "It's like plaster."

"It's like white mud."

"Stop complaining, you two," Mom said. Then her eyes went blank and she put the pot on the stove. She went to the sideboard, turned the radio down, and wrote a line in her notebook. She was writing a poem about Kettle Creek for the fall festival. She smiled at us.

"Funny little town with your feet in the mud—"

"There's not much fun in Kettle Creek," Gloria said, wandering back to the kitchen with her plate.

"—and your head lifted up to the hills—"

"Where's the rhymes, Mom?" I complained. "Miss Betts said the rhymes in the last one were all wrong."

"You tell Miss Betts," Mom said, getting snooty, "that feeling is more important than rhymes." She put her notebook in her apron and threw wood in the stove. "And a kind word is better than the strap."

"Good for you, Mom," Gloria said.

Dad came in. "Who was bombarding me?"

"The Japs came over, Dad. Didn't you notice?"

"You, eh?" He grabbed the toasting fork and pretended to bayonet me. Then he seized Mom and bent her over backward. "Let me take you away from all this." I found the way they kissed and the way he patted her, sometimes on the behind and sometimes in public, embarrassing. But I liked the way he pretended to be a romantic actor. Dad was a short man with a round belly and round face and squashed-up nose and gabby mouth. I loved to see him making fun of soppy movies.

He went to the sink and washed his hands. "Love those things in your hair," he said to Gloria.

Gloria's hands flew to her hair. "Mom," she screeched, "my curlers are still in." Mom left the stove and took them out while Gloria ate her bread and milk. Dad speared bread on the fork and started making toast. "You didn't see anyone hanging around my hearse?" he asked me.

"No," I said, alarmed, "what's in it now?"

He winked at me. "A little bit of this and a little bit of that. No cops in helmets hanging around?"

"Can you really get extra gas for it, Dad?" Gloria asked.

"If I start hauling bodies."

"You might as well," Mom said, "you've hauled everything else." She had Gloria's curlers out and she pushed her at the living room door. Then she took the toasting fork from Dad. "Pour yourself some tea."

He sat on the settee to drink it, pulling his racing form from his hip pocket. Gloria came back with her hairbrush.

"I'm late."

"Rex will do it," Mom said.

"I will not."

"I'll miss my bus."

"Lend a hand, Tarzan. No one will see," Dad said.

"Not too hard," Gloria said. She finished her breakfast while I stood behind her and set to work. Actually, I rather liked that job. She had lovely hair with a silky feeling. I combed it with my fingers as well as brushing.

"I bet Matty Yukich would like to be me."

"You shut up about Matty."

I put the brush under her hair and spread it over my hands. "Anyway," I said to Mom, "who's in the bed tonight? There's always someone sleeping in my room."

"That's what a spare bed's for, hospitality," Dad said.

"Why not hers?" meaning Gloria's.

"I couldn't very well put a man in with her," Mom said.

"What man?" Gloria said.

But Mom gave a smile and left the toasting fork on the fire grille and took her notebook from her apron pocket.

"Hush," Dad said. "Not a breath. The muse is here."

"What man?" Gloria whispered to me.

"I don't know."

Mom wrote some lines, and read: "And one dusty road to the world outside/And all the wide world's ills."

"Good stuff, Ber," Dad said.

"What man?" Gloria wasn't going to let it go.

"Mm?" Mom said. "An American."

That made me stop brushing. It changed everything.

"A pilot?" I said.

"My toast is burning!" Dad cried.

"What American?"

Mom woke up and pulled the toast out of the fire. She started scraping it with a knife. "The one I wrote away for. He was wounded and he's coming for a rest. So no pestering him," she said to me.

"Is he a pilot?"

"He's a soldier."

"Is he young?" Gloria said. "Keep brushing."

"I imagine so."

"If he was wounded he'll have the Purple Heart," I said.

Dad took his toast. "He'll need the Purple Heart if he gets toast like this."

"What's his name?"

But Mom was all business now. She took the hairbrush from me and put it on the table. She stood Gloria up and picked stray hairs off her school dress. "You get that bed cleared off, my lad. You'll find out all you need to know tonight."

That was the sort of breakfast we had — everybody running around, dancing around each other with pots and plates and kettles and pails of milk, all talking across each other, and the radio going. Food got cooked and eaten and hair got brushed and hands washed, lunches made and poems written, and we got off to school and work somehow. I was the only one who sat at the table every morning, the only one who put his spoon straight. I made a little island of order in the middle of it all, but I wasn't obsessive about it. It was just that a war was on and I was the only one who seemed to know. A war meant pulling yourself together, trying to win. All I could manage to do, in our family, was to have breakfast properly, things like that.

I went to my bedroom and cleared the bed. I kept my room tidy and clean. Things weren't thrown around. My American cigarette wrapper collection on the spare bed was neatly laid out on a tray. My BB gun was parallel to the headboard. The dresser top was equally tidy. For example, my collection of cartridge cases was arranged according to size. The pictures of fighter planes pinned on the wall were evenly spaced. Mom's broom mightn't go under the beds but when she'd finished I would borrow it and do the job myself.

So, on that morning when she first mentioned our American, I shifted my BB gun into the closet and I cleared a space for the cigarette wrappers on the dresser. I ranged the cartridge cases at the back like a row of soldiers. Then I went to the kitchen and mixed a jar lid of flour and water paste. I got Mom's scissors and cut out an American flag I'd found in a magazine. I pasted the flag on the wall above the bed where our American guest would be sleeping. Then I stood in the middle of the room and saluted it.

2

Raising the Flag

As Mom's poem said, Kettle Creek had its feet in the mud and its head in the hills. It was thirty-five miles from Auckland along a gravel road. Standing in the hills, on clay tracks cut through gorse, you could see the twice-daily bus coming from miles away through the farms. It left a trail of dust like the vapor trails jet planes leave in the sky today. Down on the flats lay the town: red roofs, wooden houses, corrugated iron stores with false fronts and curved verandas. We had no railway. We had a movie theater and a town hall, we had a park with a bandstand, and a jam factory that made no jam now that sugar was short, and some poultry farms and pig farms, and a few scrubby dairy farms like the Stewarts', some apple and pear orchards, and one or two vineyards owned by Dalmatian immigrants. We had, I guess, eight hundred people. The sea stretched away beyond the bar, where sea birds gathered at low tide. The mud of Mom's poem was in the estuary, acres of it when the tide was out. There were acres of mangroves too, an African jungle of mangroves. I can't imagine growing up without those two things—three things—mud, mangroves, warm brown tidal water.

Our house was on the edge of town, up toward the hills where the main street, Barrington Road, petered out. A hundred yards past our place it turned into a clay trail and zigzagged up toward the dam. (I hope you don't mind my saying *yards* and *miles* and *acres* and *pounds* and *ounces* and *pounds, shillings,* and *pence* instead of the *kilometers* and *kilograms* we use in New Zealand now. I'm trying to describe things the way they were.)

After I'd saluted the American flag I put my lunch in my schoolbag, and left for school. I rode my bicycle, a big heavy-framed machine with balloon tires, down Barrington Road, and shortly after I'd got off the gravel and onto the pavement, Dad passed me in the hearse and gave a honk on the horn. He had his nose stuck in the air, pretending to be an undertaker, but I wasn't amused. At home he amused me, most of the time, but outside in the world I was more often ashamed of him. He rolled on in his mock-dignified way, in the center of the road, past the jam factory, the scout hall, the movie theater, and I rode on slowly, letting him get well ahead.

"Rex," someone hissed at me (mine is a good name for

hissing). It was George Perry, by his gate. George was one of Dad's buddies, in all sorts of shady deals with him. Shady is, in fact, the word for George. (Crooked is the word for Dad, but so are lots of others—happy, eager, keen, cunning, enthusiastic, generous, acquisitive, open, honest, devious; he was full of contradictions.) George was a one-adjective person and that was *shady*. Whenever you met him he was either sidling up or sidling away, with a stoop in his shoulders that meant he didn't want to be noticed. His eyes shifted here and there, up this street, down that alley, and his voice was on soft volume all the time, a gray sort of voice—but I mustn't go on about him because he's not important in the story. I circled my bike and rode back to his gate. He pushed a scrap of paper into my hand. "Give this to Alf. In your pocket, boy, don't wave it about."

I wanted to say "Give it yourself," but I took it and put it in my pocket, and right at that moment Bob Davies, the Kettle Creek policeman, came out of the station and got into his car. George Perry turned on his feet as though in a foxtrot and slid away behind the hedge. I felt my heart turn over like a dumpling in a stew. But Davies drove off the other way, and when I looked for George again all I saw was the door of his house closing softly. I gave his gate a kick before riding on. I knew that Dad was letting us down by making deals with George Perry.

He was polishing the hearse outside the shop when I rode up. ALFRED PASCOE, GENTS' BARBER, BILLIARD PARLOR

the window said in gold letters edged with black. "Here,"
I said and gave him George's note. He read it and crowed,
"That'll never win, that's got lead hoofs."

"Dad . . ." I began.

He heard the complaint in my voice and looked at me.

"What if they catch you, Dad?"

"You reckon Bob Davies can catch me?"

Across the road two American soldiers strolled down
the walk of the Whalley house and stood at the gate light-
ing cigarettes. Faye Whalley was Gloria's friend so I knew
who they were: Marvin Varcoe and Herb Cutter from the
Ozark Mountains. That name, and their names too, had
seemed romantic until I *saw* Marvin and Herb—one flabby
and pink-colored and one with high skinny shoulders and
boil scars on his neck. They didn't come even close to my
idea of fighting men. But they gave me the chance to say to
Dad the thing that bothered me.

"Everyone else is trying to win the war."

That knocked him off balance. Dad thought it was a
game when we criticized him. Now he saw I was unhappy.
He touched my head. "I give people a bit of fun, Rex. Even
in wartime, you know, there's got to be fun." Then his
natural cheekiness came back. "And I make a bit of money
on the side." He winked at me and ruffled my hair. "Morning, boys, lovely morning," he called to the Ozark boys.
"Come and have a game of snooker later on. You can have a
free one."

I rode away to school, choosing the smoothest part of
the road. My tires were getting worn and there'd be no

more till after the war. Dad could fix me up with ordinary tires but not balloons. I put my bag in my desk and came outside to take charge of my platoon. I was NCO of the school cadets and I'd learned to shout, "Left face, right face, shoulder arms, present arms, attention, stand at ease." Not much fun. I had hoped we'd do war exercises and get something better than the broomsticks with butts attached we used as rifles. Our main job was to be an honor guard as the Union Jack went up each morning. That made me feel important and it seemed to make up for Mom and Dad not doing much for the war effort.

The whole school was lined up in classes, with the first graders on the right, wriggling and giggling and wiping their noses on the pieces of rag they had to bring, and the sixth graders on the left—the ones like me who would be off next year on the morning bus to schools in Auckland. "Platoon," I cried, "present arms!" They obeyed, with a ragged slapping of palms on rifle butts. I saluted Mr. Dent and he said, "Very good, Pascoe," with his usual clacking of false teeth. A dithery, amiable man, Mr. Dent, who should have been puttering in his garden, pruning his roses, which he loved, not trying to run a four-teacher school at the end of his days and trying to boss a fierce young woman like Miss Betts.

That was Miss Betts now, in the third- and fourth-grade room, Mr. Dent's room, striking up "God Save the King" on the school piano. I could see her fingers white as bone, whiter than the keys. She had a way of squashing keys as though they were bugs, and the tunes that came out, even

"God Save the King," were like slaps on the face. Jim Whittle, a big rough boy with flea-bitten legs, pulled on the rope to raise the flag. Up the front of the building it went, into the breeze over the gable. But halfway up the pole it stopped and Jim Whittle gave half a dozen jerks to make it move. I saw Nancy Barnhill snicker and Leo Yukich grin.

"It's stuck, sir," Jim Whittle said.

Mr. Dent, still singing, whipping up our voices with one hand, took the rope and tugged, but it wouldn't move.

"The rope's jammed in the pulley," I said.

Mr. Dent didn't know what to do. He told his class later that he felt it would be unpatriotic to pull the flag down. He dithered and tugged, and kept conducting with his other hand, and looked inside nervously at Miss Betts, who hadn't noticed anything wrong so far. It was Leo Yukich who fixed things up. I'm going to have a lot to say about Leo, because he was one of us, one of the four: me and Dawn and Leo and Jackson Coop. But before I tell you who he was, let me say how he fixed the flag. I had never taken much notice of Leo. You might say he burst upon me in that moment.

He ran to the chestnut tree beside the school and stepped up into it as though climbing stairs. Ten feet up, he ran along a branch pointing at the school and reached out his leg to the roof, curling his toes in the rain gutter for a hold. He balanced there, then used the elasticity in the branch to spring himself over. He went four-footed up the gable to the base of the flag pole, rubbed his palms on his trousers and shinnied up. The school let out an "Ooh!" Miss Betts was at the window, leaning out with her body twisted to see. If Leo fell, he'd come down the front of the school like a blade and slice her head off. But he wasn't falling, I knew that. I'd never seen anyone more sure of what he was doing.

He held the skinny top of the pole with one hand, below the cap, and worked at the pulley. "Give me a little rope, sir." Mr. Dent still had it tight but he let go. Leo unjammed the pulley by wriggling it. "Try her now." Mr. Dent pulled and the rope ran free. Everybody cheered, and Mr. Dent showed his big false choppers in a grin. But Miss Betts wasn't going to let discipline go, not even for something as exciting as this. "Silence!" she cried, and when Miss Betts made that sort of yell you froze where you were. Mr. Dent froze. Leo came down—down the pole and gable, down the tree—into deathly quiet. He walked across the asphalt to his place in the sixth-grade line.

"Yukich," Miss Betts said. He stopped. "Next time don't move unless you're told."

I couldn't believe she was saying it. I knew what Leo had done could not have been done by anyone else—well, perhaps by Rockfist or Commando Bill. It seemed heroic to me, and I felt we should be cheering him and giving him a medal. I got dizzy ten feet from the ground. When he held on with one hand and worked the pulley, I had thought I was going to black out.

"Now," said Miss Betts, "let's start again. And see if we

can do it properly." To Dent she said, "That should have been one of our boys."

She meant not a Dally, one of the boys whose families came from Dalmatia, a place in southern Europe. She meant a New Zealand boy, a British boy.

We sang "God Save the King" and marched inside to the Colonel Bogey March. Leo was still printed on my mind against the sky, on the moving clouds, on the skinny pole, making me feel weak and tummy-sick and worshipful. When we sat in class I couldn't stop glancing at him. He sat in his window seat looking bored. Once he tore a sliver from his fingernail. It must have broken in the tree. He took off his red neckerchief when Miss Betts ordered him to, and put it in his desk, giving her a steady look, not of resentment, of dislike. Miss Betts and Leo had a running fight, but though she insulted him and called him "Yuck"-ich (although she was too smart not to know the proper way to say it was "Yook," as in book) and strapped him for small things that other boys—that I—got away with, she never won. Leo just kept looking at her as though she were a blowfly he'd swat one day.

He wasn't a big boy; he was small and hard and quick. He moved twice as fast as the rest of us and had small dark eyes that seemed to see twice as much. Miss Betts always made out he was dumb, but he was bright—and so was Dawn Stewart, I believe, although Miss Betts had a game of tapping on her desk as she went by, then tapping Dawn's skull and listening as though the sounds were identical. Dawn and Leo weren't friends—neither had friends—but now and then Leo stopped boys like Jim Whittle from picking on her. Even Jim, half as big again, backed off when Leo came along.

At half past nine we heard milk crates rattling outside. "Milk's here, Miss Betts," Jim Whittle cried.

"I'm not deaf, boy." She continued writing long-division problems with her squeaky chalk. And in case you're getting the wrong idea about Miss Betts, let me say she was a good teacher. She got the facts into you and made sure you remembered them. In lots of other things, of course, she was bad. She seemed to enjoy hurting people, but that may have been because she was angry most of the time. She was angry not to be running the school. She knew she would do it better than Mr. Dent. I should add that she was good-looking too—fashionable in her clothes and the way she did her hair and put on make-up. She was a stylish pretty lady. "Sharp as tacks," Dad said. "Hard as nails," said Mom. I think she was unhappy, and that may have made her cruel. She wrote poetry, and probably did know more about rhyming than Mom—but not, I'm sure, a quarter as much about good feeling.

She turned from the board at last. "Real milk for a change." She meant by that bottled milk, not milk from Stewarts' farm, watered down some people said. Dawn kept at her work but pinkness crept into her cheeks.

"This week's monitor," Miss Betts said. I stood up.

"Choose a partner."

"Me, Rex," Jim Whittle said.

"Me," cried other boys, shooting their arms into the air. Leo was the only one who did not have his hand up.

"Leo," I said. His head came round in surprise. But he stood up quickly, glad of the chance to get out of the room. We crossed the playground to the milk shed and picked up a crate.

"Why'd you pick me?"

"Dunno," I said. I looked at the flagpole, which seemed to rotate as clouds moved by.

"I thought you didn't like Dallies."

"I never said that."

"Bettsy-bum calls us squareheads. She reckons we're pinching land while the soldiers are away."

"I don't say squareheads."

"You better not."

I had, though, said *squarehead* to Gloria when she started going out with Leo's brother Matty. I wondered if she'd told Matty, and Matty told Leo. He didn't like me, that was plain, and I looked for ways to change his mind.

"We've got a Yank coming to stay."

"I see lots of Yanks."

"Yeah?"

"They come to buy wine. With their girlfriends. In jeeps." He was dismissing me. If it hadn't been for the flagpole I'd have been angry and probably would have said something insulting, but the pole was there, over my head, and I couldn't get rid of the memory of him clinging one-handed in the sky. He noticed where I was looking.

"I can climb higher things than that."

I believed him. Still, as our arithmetic went on I began to forget him. I grew excited about my American. I wondered if he would have medals besides the Purple Heart, and what battles he'd been in, and how many Japs he had killed. I hoped he would be a lieutenant. I like the way the Yanks said "loo" instead of "lef." Lootenant Buddy Storm was the name I made up for him.

Jim Whittle made a sucking sound with his straw. Miss Betts swung around from the board.

"Was that you, Yukich?"

"No," Leo said.

"No, what?"

"No, Miss Betts."

She eyed him suspiciously. "What did you get for number four? Let me see." She walked down the row of desks to him.

"I haven't done number four yet."

She looked in his book. "You haven't even done number three. Monkeys can climb flagpoles, Yukich, but you need something up here"—knocking her knuckles on his forehead so hard the sound traveled through the room—"for arithmetic."

Whittle laughed. Miss Betts turned to Dawn. "Dawn Stewart, what did you get?"

"I haven't finished that one, Miss Betts."

"You shake yourself up, my girl, this isn't the pa." A *pa*

was a Maori village, and, of course, Dawn lived on the farm with her grandmother.

She went around the room and we kept on working. I finished the problems and started a picture on a loose sheet of paper. I got so wrapped up in it I forgot where I was. I sucked my empty bottle and made a sound louder than Jim Whittle's.

"Pascoe!" said Miss Betts, two rows away.

"Sorry, Miss Betts. It was an accident." I tried to slip my drawing under my book.

"What are you doing?" She strode around the desks at me.

"Problems," I said.

"No, boy," rapping my knuckles with her ruler, making me yelp, "under your paper."

I drew it out slowly and gave it to her: a drawing of a Yankee soldier bayonetting a Tojo-faced Jap through the middle. His speech balloon said "Die, yellow dog!"

"It's my American. He's coming to stay."

"Oh?"

"Tonight, Miss Betts. Mom wrote away for him. He might be a lootenant, I hope."

She gave a sniff that seemed to say he could have done better than the Pascoes. But she didn't strap me. "Put it away, get on with your arithmetic."

"Can I bring him to school, Miss Betts? To talk about America?"

"He might not want to come."

"I can ask him though?"

"All right, ask. Not in the mornings. After two o'clock."

"Yes, Miss Betts." I grinned around, for this was a triumph—my Yank coming to school, me getting the class off some work. All my answers were right too, when Miss Betts marked them. What a day! Only Leo Yukich wasn't impressed. He hardly spoke a word to me when we carried the milk crate back.

3

Canoe

I circled my bike around him on the road outside the school.

"Want a lift?"

He looked uncertain for a moment, then jumped on the bar. I had meant to take him as far as the turnoff to the vineyard—Kettle Creek Wines—but when I stopped at the corner he said, "Come and have a go in my canoe?"

"You bet. I better tell Dad though. I'm supposed to sweep the shop."

We rode into town. I leaned my bike on the veranda post and went inside. Dad was cutting Bob Davies's hair. He had him in the chair sheeted like a ghost and was giving him a short back and sides, taking his time so he could blarney at him about the duties of a law-abiding citizen.

He winked at me as I came in. Leo hadn't been in the shop before. His father cut his hair. The forest of lotions and creams, the range of clippers and combs and brushes on the marble-topped sideboard intrigued him. As Dad yacked on to Davies, Leo slipped by me and examined them. When he thought I wasn't looking he put his finger in the Brylcreem pot and hid a dollop in his palm.

Davies said, "You're a good barber, Alf, and a damn poor liar."

"Hey, hey," Dad said, "in front of my boy! But tell me, Bob, what harm does a little bet do? People want some fun in their lives. They need to be kings for a day, not going around with long faces"—Dad pulled one—"mustn't do this, mustn't do that. It turns our boys in blue into bogeymen, Bob. You know, I'm sometimes tempted to take up bookmaking myself, as a social service, for morale, what with Hitler and his pals around."

"Ha!" Davies said.

The Ozark boys, Marv and Herb, came in.

"Tell me, boys," Dad said, stepping away from Davies, "do I look like a liar to you?"

It startled them. "Ain't nobody calling you that," Herb said. Herb was the skinny one with boil scars.

"We came in for that free game of pool," Marvin said.

"Sure thing," Dad said. "I'll set up a table." He started for the back room, where the tables were.

"Wait a minute, Alf," Bob Davies said, "how about some oil on my hair?"

Marv, the big American—he was broad right down his

body from his shoulders to his behind, and thick-necked too, and not so flabby as I'd thought — Marv turned around. None of us had thought about how an American from the South would see Bob Davies.

"You hear that, Herb? You hear this nigra giving orders?"

"Aw, Marv, he ain't a nigra, he's a May-or-ree," Herb said.

Marv took no notice. He said to Dad, "What you cuttin' his hair for anyways? I thought this was a white man's saloon."

Dad always knew when actions were better than words. My Dad never missed a trick. Davies's mouth had dropped a little open, he was getting ready to give Marv a blast, but Dad got in before him. He spun the chair — it was one of those revolving chairs, very expensive, but Dad believed in having the best — he spun it half around until Davies was facing the Ozark boys. Then he whipped away the sheet and picked up the helmet and put it on Davies's head — and there he was, Constable Davies, in his full police uniform.

"Meet Constable Davies," Dad said.

Davies played along. With a kind of American drawl, he said, "While you're in town, you boys watch your mouths."

Well, Marv had a pink skin but now it went red. I don't think he was used to people getting the better of him. He was going to answer back, but Herb gave him a series of little shoves, like moving a stubborn cow along, and got him out of the barber shop into the pool room. I said to Leo scornfully, "The big one's fat. My one's got the Purple Heart." Leo had a huge grin on his face. He told me later on it was the best thing he'd ever seen.

Dad turned Davies back. He lifted the helmet off his head. "Southern boys. Don't know any better. I'll go in there and take their money off them."

"You leave them alone."

"Whatever you say, Bob. Oil, eh?" Instead of going to the jar he went to Leo and opened his hand and took the Brylcreem Leo had pinched, without looking at him, as though he always got it from there. Leo had not noticed the mirrors round the shop. Dad saw everything. It was Leo's turn to go red; and I was pleased the Pascoes had scored a point against him.

"Dad," I said, "I'm going out to Leo's to see his canoe. I'll sweep out later."

Dad was rubbing Brylcreem in Davies's hair. He looked at Leo sharply as we left. He hadn't recognized him till then.

"Hey, young Yukich!" Dad came after us over the sidewalk. He sent a glance inside to see that Davies was in the chair. "Tell your old man I'll be out to see him."

"All right," Leo said.

"I've got something he might like." He winked at Leo. "To sweeten his sherry."

"Da-ad," I protested.

"Nothing wrong with doing business, son." He wiped the remains of the Brylcreem in my hair and went back inside.

We rode out to Leo's past the Stewart farm, where we saw Dawn walking toward the creek, and past my Grandma and Grandpa Crombie's place. We didn't stop there. Grandma wasn't home anyway, I'd seen her in town on her motorcycle, wearing her goggles and leather helmet and leather gloves, with her white hair streaming out behind and her pink and blue floral print dress flapping on her thighs—and of course I'd looked the other way, though just as I loved Mom and Dad I loved my grandma. The sidecar of the cycle held a sack of vegetables. I guessed she was taking them to Mom. There'd be lots of greens and pumpkin in the next week. But more of Grandma later, she comes later. A lot of what I know about Dawn I learned from her.

We went past their place, saw Grandpa through the open door of his shed working on his amphibian, went whooping down the hill toward the vineyard, with me standing up on the pedals and Leo on the carrier behind, legs out wide to keep our balance. The vineyard had been a farm once and gone to scrub. Stipan Yukich, coming down from the north in the 1920s, had bought it cheap and cleared it and planted vines. Everyone had laughed at him, the Dally who thought New Zealanders would drink wine, and in a way they were right. Stipan had to make port and sherry, extra sweet, to make a living. Now, with sugar short, he was having hard times. Only the Americans kept him from going broke.

We rode up a dusty road between vine rows and came to the house, a weatherboard cottage built by the original owner. Vines on overhead trellises made a shady cavern in front of it. Leo jumped off the bike and went into a shed at the edge of the yard. Barrels on their sides lined a corridor and vats stood beyond them like giant mixing bowls.

"Dad."

Stipan and Matty were scraping out a barrel. I knew Matty because Gloria was going out with him—a good-looking boy of seventeen, a good rugby player and tennis player—and I knew Stipan by sight. But until he stood up I hadn't realized how huge he was. He was, I suppose, six foot six.

"This is Rex, Dad," Leo said. "We're going in my canoe." He added something in Dalmatian and Matty said something too. I heard Dad's name in it so he was telling Stipan who I was.

Stipan offered his hand. "How you do?"

"How *do* you do," Matty corrected kindly.

"Hallo," I said, awed by his size. My hand in his was like a matchbox in a carpenter's vise. He felt how brittle it was and didn't squeeze.

"Mr. Pascoe's coming to see you, Dad. He's got some sugar," Leo said.

Matty repeated that in Dalmatian, and grinned at me, "He's always got something, your old man."

"Where he get sugar?" Stipan's big bony face had a look of surprise.

"I don't know," I said, ashamed.

"Sugar good for sherry. Not real wine. You like wine?"

"I've never tasted it."

"Taste now."

He ran a glass from a barrel. I couldn't believe it when he offered it to me, full to the brim. He gave a little ceremonious bow of his head.

"No," I began.

"Go on," Matty said. "It's good."

"I'm not allowed."

"Have a sip. I'll drink the rest."

"I will," Leo said.

So I took the glass, and sipped, and gagged on it and almost spat it out. I'd sneaked a sip of port or sherry at home; but this was — "Sour!" I thought they were playing a joke on me.

Matty frowned. Leo was furious. "It's supposed to be like that. God, you're dumb." He looked as if he would punch me.

Stipan said sadly, "You no like? Only like sugar?" He sighed and took the glass. "I drink." He swallowed the wine in a single gulp, then went down on his knees and started scraping out the barrel again.

Leo pulled me roughly. "Come on." I knew I'd failed a test, but they were crazy, drinking stuff that was sour.

"Rex!" Matty called. I looked back. "Tell Gloria I'll be at the flicks tonight."

Leo didn't give me time to say yes. He pulled me out the back door into the sunlight. The vines stretched away in straight lines, with dark green leaves and bunches of grapes turning purple. The canoe stood upright against the back wall of the shed. It was made of canvas on a wooden frame. Two paddles poked out of it like hands. We got on either side and carried it down the drive, along the road, down the paddocks at the edge of Stewarts' farm, to a little muddy beach in the estuary. Hard work! But once launched, the canoe made everything easy. We glided over the water with shallow paddle strokes, Leo in front, me behind, heading along the edge of the cliffs and past the fringes of the mangrove jungle. It was half tide and the incoming water helped us along. The nearer mangrove trees had drowned trunks. A fizz and crackle sounded farther in, where advancing water ran into crab holes. A smell of salt and rot and ripeness hung in the air. It would have been easy to imagine crocodiles basking in the mud and snakes sliding in the crooked trunks. But Leo's mind wasn't working that way.

"Dad makes the best wine in the world."

"Sure. Okay."

"Only dumbbells don't like wine."

I had no answer to that. We paddled on.

"He used to carry sacks of gum twenty miles on his back when he was young."

I didn't know what he meant. I'd never heard of the kauri gum trade. I said, "Where's your mother?"

"She's dead." He dug his paddle in and turned us into a

side creek running up the back of Stewarts' farm. It was spooky up there. High mangroves reached down with crooked arms. The only sound was the splash of paddles. As the creek got narrower I said, "Jap subs could hide up here."

"They'd get stuck in the mud." Leo wasn't going to help me fantasize.

We went around a bend and saw a launch tied to a rotting dock. It leaned outward as though its keel was stuck at an angle in the mud.

"Who does it belong to?"

"Ma Stewart, probably," Leo said.

"Let's go on board."

"It'll probably sink."

We paddled up. It was one of those old narrow-gutted launches with high sides and a deckhouse like a roadman's hut. The paint was flaking and rot had eaten into the hull. We could just make out the name *Rose* painted on the bow.

Leo stopped paddling. "There's someone on it." We saw a face look over the bow and duck away.

"It's a Jap spy." Although, of course, I'd seen who it was.

"Sure. He came by parachute," Leo said.

We went alongside, close enough to touch it with our paddles. But as we banged and poked it Dawn stood up with one foot on the rail. She looked six or seven feet tall. She held a tin bucket full of water and she threw it at us in a sheet. I got a mouthful and nearly capsized the canoe.

"Get out," Dawn screeched. "This is my launch."

Leo was backpaddling. He'd got the worst of the water and was wetter than me. "Keep your launch. Who wants it?"

She dipped her hand in the bucket and threw a handful of watery mud at us. It freckled our shirts.

"Get out of my creek."

I tried scooping water at her with my paddle and nearly tipped us over again. Dawn laughed. She was standing on the bow barelegged with her dress tucked in her bloomers and her hair hanging over her face and she looked like the witch in *The Wizard of Oz*. She threw her bucket in—it was on a rope—and hauled up more water. We turned the canoe and got out of range.

"She's balmy. She's only a Maori anyway."

Leo turned and looked at me. "And I'm a Dally."

"I didn't say that."

He took no notice. "Okay, Stewart," he yelled, "it's your launch."

We paddled out of the creek and back to the beach. Leo said nothing on the way. "Grab it," he snarled at me when we stepped out. "Jeez, you're a weakling."

"I am not. It's got water in it."

"Well, tip it out. Not that way, dummy, the other way."

We hid the canoe in some bracken.

"You show anyone and I'll belt you," Leo said.

"Why would I show them?"

He grabbed my arm and gave me the Chinese burn.

"Ow!"

"You'll get worse than that."

"I won't show."

"I only needed you to help carry it anyway." He started off, running easily on the clay trail while I sat down and put my sandals on. I could not work out what had gone wrong but I hated Leo. I knew he would beat me in a fight—and he could climb the flag pole and he owned the canoe. The only good thing I had was my Yank. I didn't run after Leo but walked up the paddocks and collected my bike and rode to Dad's shop. On the way I started feeling better. Buddy Storm would be getting on the bus in Auckland now. Who needed Leo, who needed squareheads, when I had him?

I swept the shop and billiard room and rode home and had supper. Then I went to my bedroom and put on a fresh shirt and pants. I combed my hair. The spare bed had a clean pillowcase and clean sheets and a bedspread with fold marks from its time in the drawer. I took my picture of the Yank and Jap from my schoolbag and pinned it on the wall beside the flag.

"Rex, we'll be late," Mom called from the kitchen.

"Coming." I made a fierce bayonet lunge in imitation of Lootenant Buddy Storm.

Dad wasn't coming to the bus stop. Mom didn't think we should meet our soldier with a hearse. She and I and Gloria set out down Barrington Road. Mom had put on lipstick and a bracelet and a brooch. Gloria was wearing her best dress. I thought that showed the Pascoes knew the proper way to do things. I wished, though, we had a proper car. Buddy Storm would think we were poor. We got to the stop in front of the post office just as the bus turned into town at the other end. The sun was going down behind the hills. It made us squint across a yellow glare.

"We're going to have a lovely sunset for him," Mom said.

The bus pulled up and three or four passengers got off. Last came our American soldier. We saw his uniform moving down the aisle and his army bag bumping on his knees. He came down the steps.

I saw his face.

He was a Negro.

4

Jackson Coop

Negro was the word that we used then. *Black* was supposed to be insulting. Today it's the other way around.

He stood there all alone, with his cap in one hand and his bag in the other, feeling, I guess, that he'd come to the end of the world, our one-horse town, our single street with paddocks at the end of it and sea beyond the paddocks and then nothing but the empty sky. He looked out there and then looked at the hills, and swallowed. I saw his Adam's apple bounce. He licked his lips.

Mom stepped up to him and Gloria went a step or two, although she whispered to me, "She didn't say this." I couldn't make my feet move. I stood where I was while Mom said, "Mr. Coop? I'm Bernice Pascoe. I'm so pleased.

I thought they mightn't send you." She meant they
mightn't send a Negro to a white family.

He shifted his bag and took her offered hand awkwardly
and let it drop.

"Jackson Coop, ma'am. It sure is nice of you to invite
me." He said it with great care, as though he'd practiced it
but didn't have the words exactly right.

Mom motioned to us.

"These are my children. Gloria . . ."

Gloria shook hands with him.

". . . and Rex. Come on, Rex."

I went up to him. I didn't look in his face. I took his
hand and felt it squeeze a bit and then we both let go at the
same time.

"Howdy, Rex."

I stepped back and wiped my hand on my trouser leg. It
wasn't deliberate, I just found my hand wiping there.
Jackson Coop saw. Mom did not see.

"He's been looking forward to having you here so much.
We all have. Let's go home." Her words came in a happy
gush. "Rex, you carry Mr. Coop's bag."

"No, ma'am—"

"He's dying to, aren't you, Rex? So don't you argue,
you're our guest." She gave my elbow a push and I reached
out and took the bag and felt it jerk my shoulder down.

"It weighs some," Jackson Coop said.

"Rex is strong. Now off we go. It isn't far. You don't
mind Shanks's pony?"

"Ma'am?"

"Walking. It's an expression."

"I'm used to walking, ma'am."

Mom smiled at Gloria. "Isn't 'ma'am' nice? Come on then. Gloria on the other side so Mr. Coop won't be lonely." How merry and girlish she was. "And Rex brings up the rear. Giddy-up."

Off we went. And Rex was soon very much in the rear. The bag weighed some, as Jackson Coop had said, but it wasn't that. I did not want to be seen with them. Lopsided, I went along, and heard Mom's chatter and soft single words from "our Yank." I'd been waiting for Lootenant Buddy Storm off that bus, and look who came. A friend of Dad's who was supposedly in the know about all sorts of things had told him once that Negroes in the forces were "the scourings of the slums." He heard it from a Marine colonel. And Jackson Coop (what sort of name was that?) was only a private. I saw it, PVT, stenciled on his bag. I had no doubt he was from the slums.

Mom turned. She caught me at the moment when I'd put the bag down to change hands. "Come on, Rex."

Jackson Coop made a step toward me, as if to help, but she restrained him. "He can do it." So they went on and I gave the bag a short, hard kick before picking it up. "Nigger bag."

We walked through town. People watched as we went by. One lady ran down her path and leaned over her gate for a better view. Most of us in Kettle Creek had only seen Negroes in the movies — porters on trains, bellboys and cooks (fat ladies who were always laughing), or trumpet players in the dance band. Jackson Coop was rare — unique — like, say, one of those African animals brought to ancient Rome, an ostrich or hyena or giraffe. I don't mean we wanted to put him in an arena and make him fight, though later on it came close to that. But some of us would have liked to put him on show and walk around and prod and poke him. Not me, of course. To me he wasn't a wonder, he was a shame.

They crossed the road. I stayed on the side where I was. It took me along the sidewalk by the Whalley house and there were Marv and Herb on the porch, smoking cigarettes and drinking beer with old man Whalley.

Marv stood up. "Will you look at that?" I saw his pudgy face go strawberry-pink. He did not mean me, trudging by with a black man's bag, but Jackson Coop walking in the street with two white women and Mom's hand tucked inside his arm.

"Now I seen everything."

"Aw, Marv . . ." I did not hear how Herb restrained him, but kept on my way, falling behind, and went up Barrington Road, saw Mom and Gloria and Jackson Coop turn in at our gate and Jackson shoot a glance at the hearse. When I came into the kitchen Dad was pumping Jackson's hand.

"My wife didn't say you were a darkie. Say, I'll bet you could do with a beer."

"He hasn't had his supper yet, Alf. You must be starving, Mr. Coop."

"Jackson, ma'am. Call me Jack."

"Jack. Yes, Jack." She seemed delighted, as though by a name entirely new. "Jack is lovely. Now what do you like to eat?"

"Whatever you've got, that's fine with me."

"Snarlers," Dad said.

"We've got sausages and mashed potatoes and oodles of vegetables." Then she saw me standing in the door with the bag. "Put that on Jack's bed."

I went through the room, looking at no one, and into my bedroom, where I hoisted the bag onto the bed. Half an hour before, that bed had seemed magical because Buddy Storm was going to sleep in it. Now I wanted to jam it into the corner to get it farther away from mine. I thought, with a kind of horror, and some fear too, that I was going to share my room with a Negro. I couldn't believe Mom had done this to me.

"Private Monkeyface," I said.

I leaned across the bag and ripped my sketch from the wall — the Yank and Jap — and crumpled it up and threw it behind the dresser. Then I picked at the corner of the flag with my fingernail and pulled it off and worked it into a tiny ball.

When I went back to the kitchen, Jack was sitting at the table eating a big plate of sausages and mashed potatoes and vegetables. He held his fork the American way — but nothing was going to please me. I sat on the settee, far away from him. Dad was at the table too, being companionable. He poured himself a glass of beer and when he'd put the bottle down picked up the catsup bottle and sloshed catsup on Jack's sausages.

"Have some more. There's no shortages here."

"Alf," Mom protested, "he mightn't like catsup."

"It's all right, I do. Thank you, sir."

"Don't call me sir. I s'pose they make you darkies do that, eh? Call me Alf. The demon barber of Kettle Creek." He grinned evilly and hammed stropping a razor. Dad had been thrown a bit out of his stride by Jack and was working hard to recover. "Say, Jack, you wouldn't be in the quartermaster's department?"

"Sir?"

"Stores. Supplies."

"Now don't start that," Mom said.

"No, sir. Infantry."

"Foot sloggers, eh." Dad was disappointed.

"And no war talk," Mom said. "He's come to get away from that. What part of America do you come from, Jack?"

He swallowed a lump of sausage so he wouldn't keep her waiting. I saw it travel in his throat and saw how it hurt going down. "Chicago, ma'am."

"You ever see guys running around with tommyguns?" Dad made a *rat-tat* sound and sprayed the room with bullets. Usually I found him entertaining but he didn't entertain me that night. Jack managed to laugh.

"Let him eat, Alf," Mom said. She offered him more coffee—from a bottle of essence; we hadn't learned yet how the brown sticky stuff horrified Americans.

"No, no, what I've got is fine."

Gloria came in, dolled up for the movies. She asked Dad for two shillings and six pence and he fished automatically in his pocket.

"You're not going to the movies on Jack's first night?" Mom said.

"It's all arranged, Mom. I'm meeting Faye." And Matty too, but she didn't say that.

Jack half rose from his chair. "I've got some nylons for you ladies."

Mom pushed him down. "You finish eating. Nylons can wait."

"Real ones?" Gloria said, with that shining-eyed look girls put on for Yanks—for what they handed out more than what they were. I'd seen it before, but was disgusted to see Gloria doing it with Jack.

"The real thing," he said, and he gave a smile, a white flash of teeth in his black face.

"I can get you top money for nylons," Dad said.

"Alf!"

"I can wear them tonight," Gloria said.

"No, you can't. Tomorrow is plenty of time. The first thing Jack is doing is eating his supper. Where are you going?" That was to me, easing out of the room. I didn't want to stay there any longer.

"Homework," I muttered. My glance slid over Jack. I met his eye and realized he knew my lie. Then he forked up mashed potato and put it in his mouth and ate again.

I went to the bedroom, and didn't do homework, of course, but took my BB gun and let myself out the front door. Around on the back lawn, in the dusk, I aimed and shot, aimed and shot, at the Hitler/Tojo box, until I lost sight of the faces in the dark. I lost half a dozen BBs that night but didn't care. I knelt only five feet away and blasted holes in the enemy.

Gloria went to the movies — wearing those nylons after all; she'd got around Mom — and sat with Matty, and got the eye from Marv, she claimed next day. Faye introduced her, and Faye told her too that Marv and Herb reckoned that at home they chased niggers in their cars for fun.

"They call them nigras," Faye said. "The nigras can run."

"They wouldn't chase Jack," Gloria said.

I went to bed and read my *Champion* — Rockfist knocking out Huns with uppercuts and Bill Ross blowing up ammunition dumps. I got right away from Jackson Coop. Jackson Coop didn't exist. But in the end Mom opened the door and brought him in. His bag on the bed was open (for those nylons) but I hadn't poked in it as I might have done with Buddy Storm. I kept away, didn't even look. And I did no more than glance up when Mom brought him in.

"I'm sorry it's so small."

"It ain't small to me, ma'am. Where I grew up on the South Side we all slept in one room." He smiled at Mom, a bit self-conscious. "Eight kids in three beds."

So he came from a slum. The colonel was right.

"How awful," Mom said.

I couldn't resist it. "That's two and two-thirds a bed." The sort of smart remark I specialized in.

Jack was startled—surprised perhaps to find I had a voice. He laughed uneasily and took his toothbrush from the bag and went out with his towel. Mom was looking angrily at me.

"Don't you get smart with him. He's just a boy and he's a long way from home."

"Why'd you have to get someone like him?"

"Because I thought no one else would. And he's very nice. While he's here he's part of our family. Just you remember."

"He's not coming to school."

"Oh yes, he is. You're not wriggling out."

"Mo-om—"

"I've already told him."

Out she went and I lay there with the bottom dropped out of my world. That's a tired old metaphor. Let's see if I can find a better one. Down in Fiordland you see huge scars of rock shining in the bush on the mountainsides. The trees can't put down roots. They hold each other in place until one loses its grip and then they all go, acres of them, down into the waters of the fiord. This is called a tree avalanche. I felt as if something of that sort had happened to me. Something I'd thought surely rooted had slid away and a glistening scar was in its place.

I turned the light out, lay in the dark, and heard Jack feeling his way when he came back. I heard him taking his clothes off and folding them on the chair at the foot of his bed. Then he pulled the curtains open. (We had blackouts at that time so they couldn't be open when the lights were on.) He had stripped down to a pair of underpants and his skin glistened in the light from the moon. I watched him through half-closed eyes, thinking how easily he could kill me. He got into bed, propped the pillow up on the headboard, and lit a cigarette. His face in the light from the match had, it seemed to me, smoother shining patches than a white face would have. It went back in the shadows but when he drew on his cigarette it came out again, colored red. I was frightened. I wondered if Dad would hear me if I yelled.

He wouldn't have. Dad was off on his own affairs — down in the garage with George Perry, handing over cash for a bundle of bicycle inner tubes. He told us in the morning that Bob Davies had ridden by on his bike and shone his flashlight in and he and George had had to squat in the gap between the hood and the end wall until he was gone.

"Old George, he lost half a gallon of sweat."

They got their deal done and George crept off while Dad leaned on the fender and rolled a cigarette. He heard a girl laugh far off in the night, so he didn't light up but stood there waiting. In a moment Gloria and Matty arrived at the gate. They talked for a while, then Matty kissed her. Dad let them have one kiss. In the middle of the second he put his cigarette behind his ear and put his two forefingers in his mouth and blew an earsplitting whistle.

It came into my bedroom like a scream.

"Jeez!" Jack said. He dropped his cigarette and curled

himself down in the bed, half on his side. His hands went up and covered his head.

Dad's voice yelled, "Inside, Gloria. On your way, young Yukich."

I got out of bed and picked up Jack's cigarette from the blanket. "You don't have to be scared. It's only Dad."

Jack had his head covered the way a chimpanzee covers its head, with palms cupped on top and elbows in front as a shield. His eyes in that cave slowly came open and he listened to Gloria's feet scrunch up the walk.

"He says she's too young to go out with boys."

Jack took his arms down. He reached for his cigarette and drew on it deeply, then pulled himself up against the pillow. He let out smoke.

"How old is she?"

"Sixteen."

He looked as if he found that hard to believe. "My sisters were in the cannery when they were sixteen. Bessie had a baby of her own."

I didn't like the idea that Gloria was old enough for babies. "She's going to be a schoolteacher," I said.

He sat up more. The moonlight struck a scar on his shoulder and made it shine. "Teaching's a good job."

I looked at the scar, wondering if a bayonet had made it.

"Did you think it was the Japs when Dad whistled?"

Jack drew on his cigarette. His face shone red and went back again into the shadows. "Japs didn't whistle."

"No, I meant . . ." I made the sound of a whistling shell and drew a trajectory with my hand.

"Yeah," he said.

"Have you got a Purple Heart?"

Jack reached down and pulled his bag from under the bed. He slid his hand in and felt around and came up with the medal. He dangled it on its ribbon and gave it to me. I looked at it by the window, in the moonlight, and found it really was a heart, and purple too, with a gold border and a gold man in profile set on it.

"Who's that?"

"George Washington."

I wasn't going to show I was impressed. "Our soldiers don't get medals for just being wounded."

"That right?"

I gave him the Purple Heart and he put it in his bag and pushed it under the bed.

"If you have another cigarette," I said, "you'll have to close the curtains before you strike the match."

"I'll do that."

"There were Jap subs up north a while ago."

"Okay."

I could see I wasn't impressing him. I got into bed. "We were in the war before you."

"Sure, kid."

His face lit up, his jungle face, as he inhaled. He squashed the butt in the ashtray on the floor. He wasn't going to light up again.

I drew my blankets around me and lay there watching his scar.

5

Mammy

Getting Mom alone next morning was impossible, so I went to school knowing Jack would come to our class. I thought of hiding in the air raid trenches after lunch but I was a law-abiding boy and didn't have the nerve.

The afternoon started with English composition, which brought out Miss Betts's bossiness. She thought no one but her knew the English language, and she went around with her ruler in her hand pointing out wrong grammar and punctuation and chopping you on the knuckles for a really bad mistake. Starting a sentence with *and* was a bad mistake or ending one with a preposition. Slang was the worst mistake of all.

Chop went her ruler on Leo's hand.

"*Loony* is not a word. Nor is *gosh*."

"People say *gosh*, Miss Betts."

"Not in my class. What's this? 'Having a rotten day.' How can a day be rotten, boy? A day can't go bad. A day can't smell."

"They seem like that."

"Are you answering back?" She picked up his book to look at it and a sheet of paper fell out. Like me the day before, Leo had been drawing. But I couldn't draw to save myself—my people and cars and airplanes had to be in outline. Leo, on the other hand, had a gift. He drew landscapes full of people doing things. He drew men digging holes and women sweeping floors. He drew faces that were smiling or frowning—you could see what was going on in people's minds. On that day though, he'd done another sort. It looped away from the book and settled on the floor by my desk and I got a good look at it before Miss Betts snatched it up. It was a woman with no clothes on. She was facing away, not toward, so there was nothing rude, just her behind. Which was fat. She had fat legs. Her long hair was fanned out down her back and her arms were lifted up to hug the sun, rising over hills, very close. You could tell, somehow, that her face was smiling. I knew who it was—not just because a pumpkin was sitting at her feet.

Miss Betts held it farther from her eyes. "What's this?"

"A picture," Leo said.

"I can see that. Who is it, boy?" Did she wonder if it was her?

"I made her up." (Liar!)

"So that's what you keep in that smutty head of yours."

I don't think she was cross. I think she was amused and hiding it. Miss Betts, I suspect, had a past, and I don't believe a naked lady bothered her too much. She wasn't going to miss the chance of beating Leo though.

"Sit in your seats," she snapped at craning children.

"Follow me, Yuck-ich." She went to her drawer. "I think you need a taste of Nurse Betts." Her strap unrolled like an anteater's tongue and touched the floor.

Dawn Stewart sat two desks in front of me. I saw her hand go up. Miss Betts, holding Leo's fingertips, getting his hand just where she wanted it, did not see.

"Miss Betts."

"What is it, girl?"

"Can I leave the room?"

Someone tittered. Dawn had done this sort of thing before. She hated strapping.

"Why didn't you go at lunch time?"

"I forgot."

"You would. Be quick."

So Dawn got out—and Leo got the strap. And while we were watching, Jack must have crossed the playground and climbed the two wooden steps at the door. He found Dawn in the corridor, standing under the big picture of the King, with her head down and her hands clamped over her ears. He heard the strap and knew what it meant.

Dawn waited until she thought it was over, then looked around and saw Jack watching her. Her hands shot back as the strap cracked again.

Jack waited. He touched her shoulder. "All done."

Dawn lowered her hands.

"You okay?"

"Yes," she said. "I got to find a room with some Miss Betts."

"She's in there."

"That was a *lady* layin' into someone?" Those smacks had been so loud he'd thought they must be made by a man. "Who was gettin' it?"

"Leo Yukich."

"Not Rex, eh? You wanna take me?"

Dawn led him down the corridor, opened the door, and stepped in. We were sitting shocked. The strap always sickens. Coming down with a hiss and biting the soft skin of a hand, it turns your stomach over. Leo walked to his seat. He would not nurse his hand. Miss Betts wound up her strap, oh so neat. Suddenly, there was Dawn, making a little awkward movement backward with her hand—and my stomach gave another turn.

Jack stepped in. He was wearing a tie with his uniform and carrying his cap in his hands—and he was so black! I hadn't understood how black he was.

"Are you Miss Betts, ma'am?"

Miss Betts threw a look of amazement at me, then wiped it off as though with a washcloth. She put her strap on the table.

"Am I in the right room?" His voice, at least, was American.

"I imagine so," Miss Betts replied. "Is this your American soldier, Pascoe?"

"Yes," I mumbled.

"Well, introduce him."

"He's Private Coop."

"Private Coop. From where?"

Dawn slipped into her seat. I was having trouble with my throat. Jack answered for me.

"Chicago, ma'am."

Miss Betts nodded. "Well, do come in, Private Coop, don't just stand there." Jack advanced across the front of the room toward her table and stopped by the stove. He was working the cap in his hands and I saw his Adam's apple bounce, a movement I'd never noticed on anyone else and thought must be Negro.

"Books away," Miss Betts said. "Up straight, fingers folded." We obeyed. "Say good afternoon to Private Coop."

"Good afternoon, Private Coop." We sounded like a first-grade class.

"Hi," Jack said, and Miss Betts jerked her head at the slang. Then she smiled—inviting us into complicity.

"Private Coop, from Chicago, is going to tell us about America."

That alarmed Jack. "I'd just as soon answer questions, ma'am. I don't do much"—he searched for a word and chose her own—"tellin'."

She smiled again, and seemed to say, "Listen to how he drops his g's."

"Questions, then. Does anyone have a question for Private Coop?"

Jack stood twisting his cap. I sank deep into my seat, but there was no escaping Miss Betts.

"Pascoe. Sit up. Private Coop is your guest, so you start."

I had no question. I saw Jack's eye on me. He was asking me for help, but I had no thought for anyone but myself. All I could do was sink again, hide in my seat.

Jim Whittle shot his hand in the air. "Were you ever a slave?" One or two children laughed nervously.

Miss Betts smiled. "The slaves were freed almost a hundred years ago. Sensible questions."

"Chicago's where they have gangsters," someone said.

"And G-men."

"Do you know Al Capone?" Whittle asked.

Jack could answer that. "Bad man. I never met him."

Miss Betts took control. "What sort of people live in Chicago?"

"Ma'am, there's all sorts. There's Irish and Italians and Polacks and Swedes and Germans."

"Dalmatians?" Leo said.

"I never met none of those."

"Squareheads," Whittle said, and got his laugh.

Jack gave an uncertain grin, a little frown. "There's a whole lot of black people like me."

"What do they do? What do they work at?" Miss Betts asked.

He shook his head. "Lotsa things. They work on the

railroads and in the stockyards. In the meat works, you know, the cannery. Lotsa things."

"Perhaps Private Coop can show us Chicago on the map."

She reached behind her, pulled a cord, unrolled the world like a blind. Jack started at the rushing sound of it, or perhaps at the flashing of multi-colors—in which the red of the British Empire stood out bold.

"If you'd care to." She offered him her pointer from the table.

"Yes, ma'am." He wet his lips. "I don't get to see many maps."

"Here is the United States," Miss Betts said, tapping with her finger. We could see she was enjoying herself.

"Yes, ma'am," Jack said. "Chicago . . ." He could not get his bearings, either in our class or in the world.

"Is here," Miss Betts sweet-smiled. She took the pointer from him. "On the Great Lakes. Lake Michigan, to be precise. I always liken the Great Lakes to a hand, or a bunch of bananas, you see the shape, children? Private Coop lives on a very great lake, almost as big as the North Island of New Zealand." And he can't find it on the map, her smile said.

Leo spoiled her fun. Leo had been brooding. Looking around earlier, I had seen him licking his palm.

"Private Coop?" His voice shocked us out of the trance of delight and cruelty she had put us in. "Do Negroes still get flogged with whips?"

It did not help Jack. But it angered Miss Betts. She could not believe that Leo, after the strap, would interrupt. "You, boy! I've had enough of you." She rushed up the aisle and grabbed his ear in her fingernails. She pulled him upright, marched him to the front. With a palm in his back, she rammed him in a corner. "You wait there. I'll deal with you later." Then she looked at Jack. She would have liked to do the same to him. Instead, she turned to me.

"Pascoe. You invited Private Coop. Ask a question, boy. Toot sweet."

I said the first thing that came into my head. "How old are you?"

"I'm twenty-two," Jack said.

"Another." Miss Betts.

"Did you volunteer?"

"No. I get called up."

"Keep going."

"Do you like the war?"

"Nobody likes it. Nobody likes the chance of gettin' killed."

A shameful answer. Miss Betts gave a nasty smile. "Someone else."

Nancy Barnhill put up her hand. "Have you ever been to Hollywood?"

"I've never been there."

"Hollywood is here, in California." Miss Betts tapped the map. "Nancy?"

"It's where the film stars live. Alan Ladd and people like that. They have swimming pools—and leopards tied up on chains. Instead of dogs."

"Aw, aw." Sounds of disbelief.

"They do," Nancy cried, and looked at Miss Betts for help.

"Private Coop?" she smiled.

"I never heard nothing about no leopards."

"Nothing? No leopards?"

"I can't go to that sort of place."

"Why not?"

"Ma'am . . ." Jack said, and tapped his forefinger on the back of his hand, very plain.

"Nonsense," Miss Betts said. "The darkies of America are equal. They're treated very well since Abraham Lincoln."

Jack had been very patient. He'd been careful. He was in a strange place, feeling his way, trying to find the customs and the rules—but he'd had enough. He was sharp himself, as sharp as Miss Betts, and just as clever, though nothing we'd seen so far had suggested it. Now we saw.

Just for a moment he stood still. Then his face split open. Jack gave a watermelon grin. "Ye-es ma'am." Oh that "yes," I hear it still, mellow, rich, submissive, marvellously false. "We's happy folks, us darkies." He let his body fall with a rag-doll flop and the joints all wonky and let his head roll. He shuffled his feet and started to dance. He turned himself into a golliwog. Jack could tap-dance a little. He could tap out a simple rhythm. He went around Miss Betts in that way, floppy arms and legs but fast feet, and that sugar smile on his face. She could not move fast enough but was half a body-turn behind. She could not catch up and bring him under control. No one had ever got the better of Miss Betts, but Jack had her beaten. The fury and bewilderment of her! She could not find a way to stop him.

We stood up to see his feet. We crowded into the aisles. Boys at the back stood on desks. I stood on a desk. And at the end the door opened and Mr. Dent came in and smiled delightedly at what he took to be a concert.

Jack went down on one knee and threw his arms wide. Wasn't there a singer once, was Jolson his name, who specialized in that sort of thing? Jack did Jolson's act. He sang: "I'd walk a million miles, For one of your smiles, Ma-a-amee." And held the pose.

Mr. Dent clapped. So we all clapped, wildly. We cheered, standing on our desks. Jack stood up and dusted his knee, and gave a smile, shy, not sure again. After that Mr. Dent led him away to meet his class, and Jack had a good time with those younger kids, he told us later. Miss Betts gave a lecture, getting her own back, on how some races, Negroes, yellow people, Russian peasants, were not exactly inferior—we all, in the end, were equal before God, as the Christian Church said—but not so far advanced in developing. Brains not formed, if she might put it so, like fruit that wasn't ripe yet, crisp and ripe, but hard and green and—how should she put it?—not full of sweetness and nourishment. One day they would—well, might—be equal to the civilized races of the world. But not yet, by a long way, poor things, and we must help them and be charitable.

It did not work. She lost. Miss Betts had lost. Jack had danced around her. That answered all Miss Betts's arguments. Leo sat and grinned (she forgot to strap him again), and Dawn just looked away out the window; and I . . . well, none of her explanations worked on me. But still I wasn't ready for Jack. I was pleased he'd made a fool of Miss Betts. That was good. But Jack was not the one I had expected. And Jack was frightened of the war.

I wasn't letting him have a place.

6

Amphibian

After school Jack handed out gum in the playground. There wasn't enough to go around, but he kept Whittle and his friends at bay and made sure the younger pupils got a share. I stood with one leg over my bike and watched Jack become everyone's hero. When that was done he snatched a basketball from a girl and spun it like a top on his finger. He flicked a pass at Dawn walking by. She caught it, only just, it was so sudden, and threw it back and walked on, pulling her schoolbag over her shoulders. Jack started dribbling the ball in and out among the boys and bouncing it between his legs and behind his back. We'd never seen basketball played the American way and didn't know what he was doing, but saw his skill and went "ooh" and "aah," and cheered again when he went up and popped the ball through the hoop. At least, the others cheered. I did not.

I wheeled my bike up to him and said, "We've got to go." I did not know whether he would follow me or not but when I got out the gate and looked around there he was twenty feet behind, strolling along with Leo at his side.

"Croatians, yeah, we got them all right. Lotsa Croatian slaughtermen."

"I'm a Croatian," Leo said, "but they call us Dallies."

I fell back and told Leo we were going to visit my grandma, meaning that he needn't hang around. I hadn't forgotten yesterday. But he grinned and said he'd walk with us. Grandma's place was on the road to the vineyard. We went into town first and looked in at the shop. Dad was sitting in the barber's chair marking horses in his racing form with a pencil.

"We're going to Grandma's, Dad."

"Okey doke." He grinned at Jack. "I hope you like turnips." To Leo he said, "You tell your old man?"

"Yes."

"Tomorrow morning, eh?" And he explained to Jack, "Deliveries. If the law allows." He jerked his head up the road. Looking out the door, we saw Davies washing his car outside the police station. "Keeping an eye on me," Dad said. "Poor old Bob."

We turned back through town and passed the park. Leo had his cricket bat on his shoulder—a home-made one with the blade and handle carved out of one piece of willow. "That's the funniest lookin' baseball bat I ever see," Jack said.

"It's a cricket bat. For cricket."

"What's that?"

"You have to knock the wickets down. You hit fours and sixes," Leo said.

"What's wickets?"

"Those over there." Leo pointed at the cricket pitch. Someone had left some tea-tree wickets in place. "Do you want a hit?"

"We're going to Grandma's place. We haven't got time," I said.

Jack saluted me. "Yessir, sergeant. Permission to play ker-ricket, sir?"

I felt my face turn red. But I parked my bike and followed them onto the pitch and watched as Leo showed Jack how to hold the bat. Then he went away to bowl, and Jack at once shaped up as though for baseball. He swung cross batted and the ball rattled the stumps.

"How'd you do that?"

"A yorker. It went under your bat."

"This time I hit you out the park."

Leo bowled, Jack swung, and missed again.

It was too much for me. "You've got to keep a straight bat. You've got to keep your elbow up." I grabbed the bat and showed him.

"That looks painful."

"He's going to bowl you every time."

"Okay. Lemme try." He looked as if his arms were dislocated. Leo bowled again and Jack made a stroke.

"You had it crooked."

"I break my arms that way. Throw me a pitch," he said to Leo. "Baseball, eh?"

Leo wasn't sure what was meant but he lobbed the ball underarm at Jack, who stepped away from it and swung the bat and smacked the ball hard and high. In cricket it would have been a six. It bounced over the running track and sped down a path, passing Dawn Stewart walking home with her schoolbag on her back and a bag of groceries in her hand. She looked at it, looked back at us, walked on.

"Chuck it here," I yelled.

She took no notice.

"Come on, Stewart."

"I don't think that little girl likes you," Jack said.

It's time I told you more about Dawn. She keeps coming in, and comes in all the time from now on.

She lived on the farm with her grandmother, that tough gray stringy lady who delivered milk to Kettle Creek. Mrs. Stewart was a widow. Her husband went away to World War One and came home gassed and died soon after. Mrs. Stewart ran the farm with the help of her daughter, Rose. But Rose was a schoolgirl and Mrs. Stewart did most of the work.

It wasn't the work that broke her, my grandmother said. The work was hard and it melted her down from a plump happy lady to the sinewy person I knew, that man/woman creature in the rubber boots and plaid shirt. But no, it wasn't work, it was Rose that broke her. Mrs. Stewart hired a young man to do some fencing. It was just before the Depression. Things weren't going too badly then.

"They fell in love," Grandma said, "Rose and Jimmy. And oh, it was wonderful to see—real love. You've never seen so much kissing and cuddling. It was all so innocent and natural. How could anyone have disapproved? But the way Joan Stewart carried on, you'd have thought poor Jimmy came from Mars and had two heads and purple scales instead of skin." Jimmy was a Maori.

"Well, they ran away," Grandma said, "and I don't blame them. They took off for Auckland and Joan was all alone on her farm. It was her fault, losing Rose, but you couldn't help feeling sorry for her."

Then Jimmy died. "TB, I think," Grandma said. Rose came home with a baby. That was Dawn. Mrs. Stewart let them stay, but she made life so hard for Rose that Rose left again—and left her baby on the farm with her mother and hardly ever came back again. She lived in Auckland, sent money, sent gifts, and Mrs. Stewart took the place of mother and brought Dawn up. Most people in Kettle Creek thought she'd been treated badly and was doing a good job with the girl.

Dawn helped on the farm, as Rose had done. She helped deliver the milk. But the farm went down and down, the fence posts rotted, the paddocks grew thistle, the cowshed

rusted red and leaned to one side. In the creek the launch
Rose fell into decay. But Dawn was well looked after,
cleanly clothed, her lunches at school were no worse than
anyone else's. At home she didn't get spankings. But she
grew solitary like her grandmother. When I think of
Dawn in those days before Jack, I see her sitting in her
desk, keeping to herself; or walking alone in the playground, threading through the other girls with a neat turn
of her hip, never touching; or in the street after school with
her bag of groceries drawing one shoulder down. And, of
course, delivering the milk.

She had a photo of her mother in her drawer at home,
hidden from her grandma under clothes. She had a tiny
bottle of scent her mother had given her on her last visit,
months ago. (Her grandmother went to the back of the
farm on those visits.) She had letters in an old tin cracker
box. They started "Darling Dawnie," every one.

On the afternoon Jack played cricket and Dawn refused
to throw back our ball — refused because of me not because
of Jack — she found another letter Mrs. Stewart had left for
her on the kitchen table. She took it to her room and tore it
open. A ten-shilling note fell out. She put it on her bed
and sat beside it and read her letter. "Darling Dawnie," it
said, "How's my great big lovely girl . . ." And it said, "I
wish I could see you more often, but honey it looks as if I'll
have to go away to Wellington . . ." She saw her grandmother watching from the door. Mrs. Stewart held out her
hand with the palm up. Dawn put down the letter. She
picked up the ten-shilling note and went to the door and

put it in her grandmother's hand. She watched as Mrs. Stewart went to the kitchen, lifted the stove ring, dropped the money in, and banged the ring back hard with her poker. "There!" New bright flames showed through the cracks at the edge of the door.

Dawn went back to her room and finished the letter. She put it in the cracker box with the rest. Then she changed into her old clothes and climbed out the window and went down to the creek. She climbed through mangroves and came to the broken-down dock and the launch.

In the deckhouse Dawn had made another home. She had a table made of planks and doorless cupboards made of butter boxes. She had a cushion and a patchwork quilt. She had a mug and a plate and a knife and fork and spoon. A photo of her mother was tacked on the wall beside an old lifejacket hooked on a nail.

She sat on her cushion with her back to the wall. She took a sandwich saved from lunch from her pocket and ate it, sitting there, looking at her smiling pretty mother; and said, she told my grandma, said out loud, "Take me with you, Mom. Why don't you take me?" Tears got in her sandwich later on, but it was only Marmite so it didn't matter much.

While Dawn was at the launch, Jack and I and Leo arrived at Grandma's. It's odd how I say "Grandma's" because I had a Grandpa too and he wasn't someone you could overlook. But Grandma was the one you noticed first. Grandma was unforgettable.

I leaned my bike on the front porch and led the others down the path at the side of the house, past the shed that housed the motorcycle. This machine, a Harley Davidson, had a sidecar, and Grandma sped around Kettle Creek on it with a sack of vegetables sitting up beside her like a fat old pumpkin-headed passenger. Grandma was the nearest I ever saw to Rockfist Rogan, except that she wore dresses on her machine. How she embarrassed me and how I loved her!

Her garden was walled by coalsacks nailed to tea-tree posts. Beans overreaching their poles waved at the top and squash and cucumber vines crept out the bottom.

"Wait here," I told Leo and Jack. I unhooked the coal-sack door from its nail and stepped in, advanced down a lane with tomatoes on one side and silver beets on the other. Grandma's garden affected me differently each time. I might hear growth humming and roots drinking and sap running and fat leaves creaking as they turned to follow the sun, and might start humming myself and feeling my own sap rising in my limbs. Or I might see tendrils reaching and long squashes like pythons curled in the shade and feel that I was threatened, food for them. Or I might imagine myself in Africa and put my foot on a pumpkin, a beast I'd shot. Or simply be hungry—pick a tomato, crunch a butter bean. And always I had to warn Grandma I was approaching.

"Grandma," I said.

"Who's that?" She was behind a bean row.

"Have you got your clothes on, Grandma?"

I saw a naked arm go up and pluck a hanging dress from a pole. It fluttered in the green jungle as she pulled it on. "Rex, dear," Grandma said, coming into the path, advancing to kiss me. Her dress was one of her old baggy multicolored ones. I often thought she'd look better in sacks. She wore laceless canvas shoes with her big toes breaking out and a tennis eyeshade casting green light on her face. Her long white hair hung down her back. My hands got tangled in it as I kissed her.

"All right," I called, "you can come in."

Jack and Leo came through the opening, along the path, single file. I saw their eyes go darting from side to side.

"Grandma, this is Private Coop, from Chicago."

"Jackson, ma'am. Call me Jack."

"Hello, Jack." They shook hands.

"And Leo," I said. "From the vineyard."

Grandma tapped a finger on his head. "This young man I know. You peeked in my garden this morning so you could see an old lady worshiping the sun."

Leo went red. The hand Miss Betts had strapped opened and shut. But Grandma wasn't really angry with him. "What did your father think of my parsnip wine?"

"He liked it," Leo said. I could tell he was lying.

"Well, you boys pick yourselves a tomato. There's no spray, so they won't poison you." She turned to Jack. "What do you think of my garden, Jack?"

"I've never seen anyplace like it. I've never seen pumpkins so big." I saw how it affected him—a wonderland.

"Tomato?"

"Yes, ma'am."

"There's no mystery, Jack. Sun and pure water and natural manure. Cow dung's best. Let nature do the work." She lectured him as he ate tomatoes, one, two, three, squirting seeds on his army shirt. Leo and I picked beans into a bucket, then tagged along as she took him to the end of the garden to show off her compost heap. Grandma was known in Kettle Creek as the Compost Queen! She heard it as a title of respect.

"See the richness." She held out a handful. "Smell it."

"Yeah, good." I don't know what he really thought. It wasn't a bad smell, but you had to be Grandma to find it sweet. She plunged her arm in, up to the elbow.

"Feel the warmth. Roll up your sleeve."

Jack obeyed. He pushed his arm into the compost, uncertain at first. Then his eyes widened. "It's hot."

"That's nature cooking good things for herself."

"It's warm as my blood."

Grandma pulled her arm out. She stepped into a lean-to beside the heap and in the dark and damp there lifted sacks. "Come and see."

I was ready to slink away if Grandma made a fool of herself. At the same time I told myself we didn't have to care what Jackson Coop thought; he was no one. Grandma set the sacks aside and displayed her worms. There were thousands of them, inch-long, pink and shiny, a spaghetti farm. She scooped up a handful.

"Don't let anyone tell you that the dog is man's best friend. Want to hold them?"

"I don't mind," Jack said, swallowing.

She put a dollop of worms in his hand and he grinned uneasily. Their coldness, after the compost, must have been a shock.

"Each one of those is a little factory of nutrients," Grandma said.

"Yeah," Jack said, "they workin' hard."

"They will be when they get in the ground," Grandma smiled. "Sunlight, Jack. Compost. Worms. Pure water. It's not a very long list, the things we need."

"No, ma'am." She amused him but he liked her. He stood there with his handful of wriggling worms and took deep breaths of the sunny compost-scented air, smiled at her and liked her and looked as if he had found a home.

I did not care for that.

"Is Grandpa in his workshop?" I said.

"Yes, yes, come and meet Freddie," Grandma cried.

Jack put down his worms and we trooped out of the garden. Grandpa's workshop was around the other side of the house beside an outlying paddock of Stewarts' farm. It was a patchwork of iron sheets, each at a different stage of rusting away. Once it had been a garage and carpenter's shop but these days Grandpa built inventions there. He had invented a machine for making concrete blocks and a machine for digging trenches—half built them, then abandoned them. Now he was busy on the one he described as "my best yet." I thought so too. I really wanted him to finish it.

He looked up wildly as we came in the door.

"Freddie, this is Jack. Bernice's American," Grandma said.

"I can't turn this nut."

He was a small spry man, seventy in that year of '43, but behaving like twenty-two. He wore khaki shorts that bagged over his skimpy behind, a torn undershirt, horribly oil-smeared, a beret stiff with grease, and dusty cloudy speckled spectacles. I've never worked out how he saw through them.

He did not offer to shake Jack's hand but demanded, "Do you know anything about engines?"

"Some," Jack said. He approached and peered in. "Man, you got trouble in there."

"What is it?" Leo asked me.

"An amphibian. It's supposed to go on land and water."

"Lemme have a go with that wrench," Jack said.

"Spanner," I corrected him.

"Yeah, spanner." He took it from Grandpa and freed the nut.

"What's it for?" Leo said.

"Getting wounded men off beaches." I thought the machine was beautiful, and the idea of it beautiful too. Its double purpose intoxicated me. As Jack and Grandpa worked in the engine I toured Leo around it—and I have to say now that a more jerry-built makeshift machine was never constructed. The boat part of it was a clinker-built dinghy, twelve feet long. It sat down low on a light chassis, with four solid rubber tires looking very naked out at the sides. I never understood the transmission system or the belt arrangement that fed power to the propeller shaft. Mechanics didn't interest me. The engine worked, the wheels turned, that was all that counted. And out the back a propeller stuck like a child's toy; yet I had no doubt it would whiz the amphibian along at twenty knots.

"Grandpa says I can put my BB gun on the front."

Jack looked up from the motor. "Then the other side shoot at you."

I looked at him with contempt. Of course they would. That was war. But they wouldn't get me, I'd get them, I'd mow them down. I saw myself in the amphib, speeding at a beach with machine-gun rattling, then roaring up the sand with no loss of speed, and Japs in the trees falling over and lying dead. Saving wounded men wasn't my idea of war. I jumped into the dinghy, making it bounce. Grandpa jerked his hand out of the engine and nursed his thumb, looking crossly at me, and Jack waited till I settled down. I stood on the bow seat, swinging my Lewis gun, winning the war.

"What's this for?" Jack asked Grandpa.

"Ah, that's my gearing system, for the propeller. I'm patenting that."

"I've seen some things . . ." Jack put his face deep in the motor and studied whatever it was from an inch away. "I guess it could work."

"You think so?" Grandpa was pleased.

"You might have some trouble here, though."

"Yes, that's a bit of a puzzle, bypassing that."

They poked and peered, unscrewed this and that, while Leo and Grandma watched over their shoulders. They took no notice of me in the bow, spraying bullets. I looked around and saw them clustered there.

Grandma had her hand on Jack's arm as she stood on tiptoe to see. It was only then I realized I was left out.

7

Dawn Has Visitors

Grandma gave us scrubbed carrots to eat, and Leo and I
took Jack down to the mangroves to see the canoe. Leo ran
ahead.

"It's gone," I heard him shout.

I ran to join him. Flattened bracken showed where it
had been. We hunted around. Leo's face was white. He
kept on throwing looks at me.

"I didn't take it."

"Who did?"

"Dawn Stewart, I'll bet."

Jack arrived.

"Someone's swiped my canoe."

"Dawn Stewart," I said. I had no doubts.

"Okay, let's get her," Leo said.

We headed off along the bottom of the cliff, above the tideline, through mangroves that were stunted and dry, leaving Jack to find his own way. We climbed up a bank into a paddock and ran along the edge of a clump of trees and came to the place where the mangrove swamp curved into Stewarts' farm.

"In here."

We climbed a barbed-wire fence with sacks wrapped round the barbs and followed a path through scrub and mangroves. The path angled off along planks laid on the mud, but a climbing way showed in the trees. We saw muddy footmarks on the branches and followed those. The broken-down dock appeared, and then the launch, leaning to one side. We jumped on to the dock.

"Stewart," we yelled.

She was there at once. "You get out."

"You swiped my canoe."

"I did not."

We picked our way along the rotten planks. Dawn had her bucket ready. She had a way of throwing that spread the water in a sheet. We almost lost our footing as it hit us, and by the time we'd recovered she had dipped the bucket in the creek and was holding it ready again.

"Get out."

"I want my canoe."

"I haven't got it." Then her eyes looked past us. Leaves rattled and feet hit the dock. Jack had arrived. He stood politely, with his cap in his hand.

"Howdy, ma'am. That's a nice launch you've got there."

Calling her *ma'am*! Dawn Stewart! Again I looked at him with contempt. "She stole Leo's canoe."

He took no notice but smiled at Dawn. "Mind if I come on board?" He picked his way past us on the planks. She lowered her bucket. "Only you. Not them." She raised it again as we edged closer. Jack stepped over the rail and stood on the deck.

"I'll keep an eye on them. They'll behave. Hey, this is great. Does the engine go?"

"Not anymore." She watched angrily as Leo and I climbed on. "This is *my* place."

"Where's my canoe?" Leo said.

"How would I know?"

"You pinched it, Stewart," I said.

"Hey, hey!" Jack lifted a hand.

"She did."

"Well, she says no. You always got to believe what a lady says. That's good manners." He strolled on the deck and looked down the creek, then smiled at Dawn. I saw, with some puzzlement, that he was happy. What was there here to be happy about?

"Thank you," he said, "for letting us come on board. We won't come back again unless you invite us."

His courtesy made Dawn blink. She put down the bucket. "*You* can come," she said, with a look at us that made it plain we couldn't.

"Who cares?"

"Where's my canoe?"

Jack took no notice. He looked at the deckhouse. "That your house in there?"

"Yes."

"You mind a visitor, ma'am?"

"As long as they stay out."

But Leo and I looked in from the door. We saw the table and cupboards and cushion and quilt and concealed our approval. Jack still held his cap in his hand. He stood as though in someone's front parlor and smiled at Dawn. "Nice house."

She kept her sharp elbow in the door, barring us. He saw the photograph tacked on the wall.

"That's a real nice lookin' lady." He looked from it to her, then back again. "Your mother, eh?"

"Yes," Dawn said.

"She's real nice lookin'." Dawn stepped away from the door. She was pleased by his compliment but stayed offhand. "This launch is named after her. My grandma named it."

"Rose," Jack said. He must have read the name from the bow.

Dawn was surprised. "Yes," she said.

He smiled at her. "Your daddy must be a May-or-ree, eh?"

That made me, at the door, give a snicker. Jack turned his eye on me. It was cold.

"Yes," Dawn said, "he was."

Jack picked up the *was* and looked back at her. "Your daddy's dead?"

"When I was a baby," Dawn said.

"So it's you and your mammy and your grandma?"

Dawn shook her head. Her eyes slid away. "My mother's not here. She works in Auckland."

Jack nodded. He turned and looked around the deckhouse again. Then he smiled and touched her arm. "That's a real pretty color. Lena Horne's that color."

Dawn went pink under her brown. And right there Dawn became his friend. I saw it happen. And Leo Yukich was his friend already. And so were Mom and Dad and Gloria and Grandma and Grandpa. I was the only one who wouldn't like Jack. It took me a little longer yet.

Dawn gave him an apple and we stayed on the launch while he ate it. I had another dig or two at her about the canoe. She kept on denying she'd taken it and Jack said, "Hey, leave it be."

"We'll look for it tomorrow," Leo said. I agreed to meet him after school. He jumped onto the dock and climbed away through the mangroves. Jack and I walked up through the farm at Dawn's invitation—rather, she invited him and I tagged along. I should have headed off to pick up my bike but I was beginning to be possessive. Everyone else seemed to be grabbing Jack and although I might not like him he still belonged to me.

"Them's cows for milking?" Jack said.

Mrs. Stewart was herding them into the yard. I noticed Dawn grow nervous as we approached. When she saw us

Mrs. Stewart stopped short. It was as though she'd got one of those pains that stand you still for fear of making them worse.

We walked up the other side of a fence. "Grandma, this is Jackson Coop from America," Dawn said.

Jack put his hand over the fence. "Hello, ma'am."

She made no move to take it. "Close that gate," she said to Dawn.

"Yes, Grandma." Dawn climbed the fence and closed the gate behind the cows.

"I don't let people on my farm."

"I'm sorry," Jack began, but Dawn was back.

"It was a short cut, Grandma. I said they could."

"Well, they can't. It scares the cows."

Even Jack could see that was a lie. But he didn't know what to say and I felt I had to protect him. "He's one of our allies. He's been wounded."

He stopped me with a hand on my shoulder. "I'm sorry, ma'am. We'll be on our way."

"The gate's up there."

Jack nodded politely. He put on his cap and gave a small salute at Dawn. "Come on, Rex."

"She can't talk like that."

"You reckon?"

"You're a soldier."

"That don't make any difference. Main thing," he whispered, "we don't make any trouble for that girl."

I looked for Dawn but she was hidden by the cows. Perhaps she had bent down to hide herself. We passed around the side of a wooden shed, both barn and workshop, filled with the junk of thirty years of unsuccessful farming.

"Watch out for the dogs."

Two underfed mongrels, part collie, part mastiff perhaps, strained and leaped at the end of their chains. Their bare teeth, laid-back ears, and matted coats turned them from farm dogs into wolves.

"They'll bite," I warned. Since he didn't know cows, I thought he mightn't know dogs.

Jack walked up to them. "Ain't no puppy dogs sceerin' Jackson Coop." He was putting on his happy Negro act. The dogs went into a frenzy of snarls, but he stepped into the range of their teeth and suddenly they were still, sniffing the hand he offered them. He tousled their ears and necks. "Jus' gotta show them you ain't sceered." The dogs whined. "We're buddies now, ain't that so?" They wagged their tails and seemed to agree.

"Give 'em a pat." I put out my hand and touched their heads, even though they stiffened and stopped their wagging.

"That lady there, she ain't so friendly as her dogs."

"No."

"Well, we best keep out of her way."

We walked up the drive.

"You like some gum?"

I hesitated.

"Saved some for you."

"All right. Thank you."

I took it, unwrapped it, put it in my mouth. Jack and I

went on to the road and around to Grandma's for my bike.
We talked of this and that—worms, canoes, dogs, cricket,
baseball—as we went. I began to see he wasn't the person I
had thought he was. I had to go right back to the beginning and meet him again and go on from there.

I'm surprised he was so patient with me.

8

Sugar

I'm the only one who knows the truth about the great sugar mystery. Jack told me, and I promised never to tell. I've kept my promise until now, but this is Jack's story so I have to put it in. Dad puzzled over it for years and came pretty close to the truth now and then.

It happened the morning after our visit to the launch. Dad had two sacks of black-market sugar under a tarpaulin in the hearse and was taking them to Stipan Yukich, who, he was sure, would pay a good price. He let me put my bike in the back of the hearse for a ride to school and I lifted an edge of the tarpaulin and saw the sacks. I felt sick. Dad was being crooked again. He was being careless as well. Driving through town with sugar! He should have been caught a dozen times over.

Jack was going with him for the ride. He didn't know what was under the tarp. We stopped outside the school and lifted my bike out. Dad got alarmed at the children around the hearse.

"Watch those doors! If you get inside you go to the cemetery."

Jack waved at all the friends he'd made the day before. Off they went, Dad tooting—and if I'd watched a bit longer I would have seen Bob Davies in his car following them. But I turned away, found Leo, gave him the Hershey bar Jack had sent—"Don't let Bettsy-bum see"—and gave Dawn hers.

"He showed me his Purple Heart," I told kids crowding around. "He's got a big scar, right across his chest. From a Jap bayonet." I made up that last part.

Meanwhile Jack and Dad drove to the vineyard. Jack noticed a black car, way back, but had no reason to think it was following them. My guess is that Davies overheard some of what Dad said to Leo outside the barbershop— heard a little, put two and two together, watched and waited. His great ambition was to catch Dad—black marketing, bookmaking, he didn't care. But although Bob Davies was a good country cop, he wasn't a very good detective. He should have stopped the hearse and searched it and arrested Dad. Instead he followed, hoping perhaps to get Stipan Yukich too.

The hearse rolled into the vineyard and stopped outside the shed and Dad played "Come to the cookhouse door, boys" on the horn. That was his way, always flamboyant. Stipan and Matty came out of the shed. "Mr. Yukich." Dad bounced up to him. "You get my message?"

"Message?" Stipan looked blank. He turned to Matty. "Sugar, Dad," Matty said, and added something in Dalmatian.

"The sweet stuff," Dad said.

Jack came around the hearse. "This is my friend Colonel Coop from the U.S.A."

"I ain't no colonel," Jack said. He shook hands with Matty and Stipan and even his big hand was swallowed in Stipan's.

"Come here," Dad said. "Got something to show you." He went to the back of the hearse and threw the doors open. He leaned in with a grin and flipped the tarpaulin. "Presto! Sugar!" Dad loved this sort of playacting. "That's special delivery, just for you."

"Where you get?" Stipan asked.

Dad waved his finger waggishly. "Mustn't ask. Just let's say I've had my scouts out scouring the country." But he made a sideways wink and a jerk of his head, implying that Jack was the supplier. It alarmed Jack. He'd caught on right away that the sugar was illegal and he wanted nothing to do with it. A U.S. soldier caught in criminal dealings in New Zealand would be in serious trouble. Trust Dad not to think of that. He was always getting people into sticky situations—quite by accident, of course.

"You could make a nice lot of sherry with that. For our Yankee friends. And their little girlies with the sweet tooth, eh?"

Stipan spoke Dalmatian to Matty again, asking if the sugar was stolen, and Matty—he told me later—answered that Dad wouldn't steal but must have got it from a crook somewhere. He said *crook* in English; and Stipan said, "Crook?"

"Hey, nothing's crooked, I'm a businessman," Dad said.

Matty was in an awkward position. Remember, he was sweet on Gloria. "Not you, Mr. Pascoe. Someone else."

"I no want," Stipan said.

"Steve, of course you want. Where can you get sugar?" His eyes went flickety-flick, Stipan to Matty, back again. "I'll give you a good price."

"What if the police come?" Matty said.

Dad laughed. "Bob Davies? I could bring a truckload of sugar in here and he'd think it was horse manure."

I wonder if Davies heard. He hadn't driven in—which he should have done—but parked up the road and sneaked through the vines. Matty found his footprints later on. He crouched there, watching, waiting for the business to be done. Then he'd pounce. He must have been furious when Stipan stepped back from the tail of the hearse.

"I no want. You take away." He went back into the shed, leaving Dad openmouthed.

"What's the matter with him?"

"I'm sorry, Mr. Pascoe," Matty said, "Dad's not going to break the law."

"Bend it. Bend it is all I do."

"Come on, Alf," Jack said. He closed the hearse doors and made Dad get in the driver's seat. Davies should have stepped into the yard then. He still had Dad redhanded. Instead, he chose to follow again. Maybe he thought Dad would try another customer.

Back to town the hearse went, Dad talking all the way, and when they turned into Barrington Road Jack noticed the black car again. He said nothing to Dad but asked to be let out at the grocery store. He had a shopping list from Mom. Dad let him out and Jack watched from just inside the door. The hearse turned down the alley to the yard behind the poolroom, and sure enough, the black car turned down too, slow and sneaky; and that was a policeman at the wheel.

Jack moved fast out of the store without the grocer seeing. He'd grown up on the streets of Chicago. He could cross a public road invisibly and slide down an alley like a cat. When he got to the corner and looked around, Bob Davies had just got out of his car. No sign of Dad. Dad had gone through to the barber shop.

Davies had parked his car so the hearse could not get out. He opened the back doors—Dad careless again—and lifted the tarp and looked at the sugar. Grinned like a wolf. He cracked his finger joints, set his helmet straight, and marched into the poolroom for his prey.

Jack reckoned he had only half a minute. Davies had left the hearse doors open and that saved a second or two. He ran to the hearse, pulled the heavy sacks, one with each hand, to the tail, hefted them up, an arm for each, and ran under that heavy load to the only hiding place Davies wouldn't think of. He stowed them there. Then it was back up the alley, across the road, ambling casually, and into the grocer's, where he stepped from behind a rack of seeds as though he'd been there all the time. He took Mom's shopping list from his pocket. "Howdy, sir." He smiled at the grocer. "You got some sugar? Mrs. Pascoe give me these here coupons."

Oh yes, Jack knew his way around.

The next part of the story comes from Dad. He was tying on his apron when Davies came in from the pool-room.

"Morning, Alf."

"Bob. You gave me a heart attack." Dad wasn't joking. His heart flipped right over, he said.

"Come with me a minute, eh? There's something I want you to see."

He took Dad through the poolroom and into the yard, keeping close to him all the way. "I think he expected me to run for it." Dad must have been tempted. The doors of the hearse were open wide. "My mouth was so dry it was like eating green persimmons."

Davies didn't look in the hearse. He pointed inside but kept his eyes on Dad, wanting to enjoy every minute. "What would those be, Alf?"

Dad looked. At first he thought Davies was playing cat-and-mouse with him. His eyes went darting about, looking for where the sugar might be.

"What's what, Bob?"

"Quit playing games. I've got you, Alf." Then he looked.

"Poor guy," Dad would say, telling the story. He felt sorry for Bob Davies. "He looked as if Joe Louis had punched him in the gut. He looked as if he was going to cry."

Davies hunted of course — under the hearse, in the poolroom, in the sheds opening off the yard. He even got a ladder and climbed on the roof.

"You've been seeing things, Bob."

In the end there was nothing for him to do but go home. He drove out of the alley and up the road — and Jack, who had spent half an hour chatting with the grocer, came out of the door at that moment, with Mom's groceries. Later on, when Davies asked, the grocer swore that Jack had come into his shop when Dad had dropped him and not left it for half an hour. Jack was a slick mover, as I said. Davies got no satisfaction.

Where was the sugar? Why, in the trunk of Davies's car. When he arrived back at the station and opened up to take out some equipment, there were the two sacks, fat and bland. There wasn't a thing Bob Davies could do about it.

"Gone!" Dad said. "Vanished into thin air," with a look at Jack.

"Don't look at me," Jack said. "I was in the grocery store all the time."

But he told me, "I couldn't let your daddy get caught. He's been good to me."

Jack spent a lot of time with Grandma and Grandpa. He helped with the amphibian but liked even more working in the garden, spreading compost, digging potatoes, picking beans and cucumbers. He pulled out old tomato vines and turned the earth over and held up huge worms for Grandma to see. He wheeled the barrow in the cow paddocks of Stewarts' farm while she scooped up shovelfuls of manure.

"How's Rex getting on?" Grandma said.

"He's doing okay. He didn't expect anyone like me."

"He thought you'd be Errol Flynn, with a chestful of medals." (Errol Flynn, a swashbuckling actor.)

"Yeah," Jack laughed. Then, curious: "Why did Mrs. Pascoe invite me?"

"She likes Paul Robeson." (Paul Robeson, a Negro actor and singer.)

Grandma lifted a dry cowpat and showed Jack threadlike worms on its underside. Perhaps they reminded her of me, because she said, "Rex is not a bad boy. He just wants to win the war, all by himself. He thinks his mom and dad aren't trying hard enough."

"Yeah, that Alf. He wouldn't last half an hour in Chicago."

"He wouldn't last half an hour in Auckland. Kettle Creek is Alf's size; he can just about handle it."

"I'd like to come back to Kettle Creek," Jack said.

"Don't be too sure." She pointed at Mrs. Stewart, striding over the paddocks.

"Who said you could come on my land?"

"Lay off, Joan, I've been getting cow dung here for twenty years," Grandma said.

"You can come, not anyone else."

Grandma winked at Jack. She knew better than to introduce him. "Anyway, we've got enough. Oh, Joan, those old scales you used to have, can I borrow them? For the veggies I'm taking to the festival? Ask young Dawn to drop them over. Perhaps she'd like to help in my booth?"

And off she went, with her shovel on her shoulder and Jack at her side with the barrow. Grandma could get most things she wanted. She could handle Mrs. Stewart, up to a point. As they unloaded the dung in the garden, she told Jack the story of the Stewart farm, Rose and Jimmy, Dawn's childhood.

"Joan does her best. She keeps the girl looking nice, that sort of thing." It wasn't enough. And here I'd better say that Grandma and Dawn had a friendship I knew nothing about. Dawn used to walk across the paddocks and spend half an hour talking to Grandma. That afternoon when she brought the scales, Grandma hunted through a box of old photographs and found a photo from 1910. It showed two women in white dresses holding racquets by a tennis net and smiling, smiling, with white shining teeth. One of them was a pretty girl.

"Is this my grandmother?"

"Yep."

"She's smiling," Dawn said.

"Of course. She was young. She was happy."

"Could she play tennis?"

"I'll say she could. She was deadly at the net. Quick as a cat." She fetched another box, junk this time, not photographs, and upended it on the mat. Searched in the bric-a-brac. Found a tiny silver-plated cup and dusted it on her sleeve. "We won the ladies' doubles in 1910."

Dawn took the cup and puzzled out the names. "Miss J. McInnes. That was her?"

"Joan McInnes. See, in the photo, her engagement ring?"

"What happened?"

"Ah, too many things." Far too much for anyone to explain. "Would you like to have that photograph?"

"Yes, I'd love it. She said I can help on your stall."

"Good," Grandma said. "Take a bag of veggies home to her."

Dawn carried them home and put them on the table. She hid the tennis photo in the drawer with the bottle of perfume and the photo of her mother, and looked at it frequently in the days that followed, trying to work out the puzzle—how could Miss J. McInnes be so happy then and Grandma Stewart so unhappy now?

9

Chicago

Leo and I searched for the canoe but couldn't find it.

"It could be Whittle and his gang."

"They don't come here. I still say it's her."

We called Jack from Grandma's garden and went to the launch. Dawn was swimming in the creek and she stayed in the mangroves on the other side while we changed. Jack wore Dad's 1920s bathing suit, which was tight around his chest but baggy at his hips.

Dawn was a better swimmer than Leo and me. She dived off the bow and didn't come up, didn't come up . . . and Jack's head went this way and that, looking for her. "Hey," he said taking a step and stopping, then taking another.

"She's swimming under water." But I wasn't sure.

Dawn surfaced twenty yards away. "Come on, yeller bellies." She was completely changed from the girl at school.

Leo and I dived in and tried to reach her but came up short. Jack sat on the rail.

"Come on, Jack."

"I can't swim."

I couldn't believe it. We were river kids. We swam almost as soon as we could walk. Dawn duck-dived and came up by the launch. Her sense of direction was amazing. You couldn't open your eyes in that yellow-brown water. She grabbed Jack's leg and tried to pull him in. He let himself go but twisted around and held the rail. Leo caught his other leg.

"No. Hey. Leave go." I saw the panic in his eyes.

"It's not deep. Come 'round the stern."

He went hand over hand where I showed him and stood in water up to his waist.

"We'll teach you."

Dawn and Leo had swum off. They wriggled into the mangrove trunks and dipped for handfuls of mud and pelted each other.

"Let yourself float." I was offhand with him. I thought it shameful that a grown man couldn't swim. "Now try dog-paddling, like this."

He tried and almost sank and reared up in a half-panic.

"Keep your fingers closed."

Leo threw mud at us.

"Lay off, I'm teaching him."

Dawn threw and hit Jack. Mud stuck on the scar that ran like a ragged sword from the point of his shoulder into his chest. He scraped it off and threw it back. The time wasn't right for lessons. I watched sourly as Jack climbed into the mangroves, hunting Dawn and Leo. They splattered him with mud, and he, dipping down, came up with great handfuls and threw back. It was too good to stay out of. I went plowing in and a mud fight raged, Jack and me against Dawn and Leo. We drove them back but they split up and took us from the sides. Up and down the edge of the mangroves we went, all of us plastered an inch-thick with mud. No side won. In the end everyone threw at everyone else. We washed ourselves clean by diving deep—Dawn and Leo and I—and poured buckets of water on Jack as he stood at the stern of the launch. Then we dried off on the warm deck.

"How come you can't swim?"

"Ain't no swimming pools where I come from."

"There's a lake."

"I've only seen that lake two, three times."

I found that hard to believe: a lake as big as the North Island that you hardly ever saw.

"When it gets hot, maybe someone opens the fire hydrant, us kids cool off under there."

"That would be fun," Dawn said.

"Yeah, fun." He smiled at her. Jack was patient with us all.

"What's your place like?" Leo asked.

"My place?"

"Your house? Where you live?"

"I don't have no house. My mammy, she's got two rooms. In a tenement house." He measured with his hands and grinned. "With big rats instead of puppy dogs."

"Yah," Leo said, "that's more than a foot."

"I'm tellin' you."

"Was it a slum?" Dawn spoke the word apologetically. We'd heard about slums from Miss Betts.

"Yeah, a slum."

That kept us quiet. Leo said, "What about your job?"

"I don't have no job. I learn about cars though. I wash cars and look in the motors. Learn that way. Washin' cars, that's better than the stockyards." We sat while he thought about Chicago. He shrugged his shoulders, putting some memory aside. "Then I went to be a boxer, at the gym."

Too bad he said that. I was starting to see a real Jack but now, in a flash, put an unreal one in his place.

"Did you have any fights?"

Jack gave me a lazy look, half amused. "I got my head beat off."

"Did you win any, though?"

"One or two."

"By knockouts?"

"I knock one feller out—"

"Great!"

"—one feller knock me out. Ain't no future. I'll try for a mechanic after the war. Then maybe I can come back and get me a job in Kettle Creek."

"Yeah," said Leo.

"Yeah," said Dawn. They liked that. But all I could see was Jack knocking another boxer out.

"An uppercut?"

"I dunno, Rex. I jus' kinda swing my fist an' down he go."

I thought he was being modest. We got dressed and I made some collections for Dad while Jack waited. At half past five we stopped at the barber shop. Dad was out the back practicing shots at a pool table. I gave him the money and he opened up the wall seat and unpadlocked a tin strongbox lying on its back—his place for spare cash and the betting ledger. He kept only one book so he could get rid of it quickly in emergencies.

"George Perry didn't want to pay."

"George never wants to pay. He gets around here like Phar Lap when he has a win."

I watched Dad count the money and put it away.

"Jack's been a boxer."

"You don't say."

"He's won some fights by knockouts."

"And lost some too," Jack said. He was idly rolling balls into the pockets.

Dad threw a speculative look at him. I guess right there he started working out a use for Jack. But all he said was "Don't talk about losing, it's bad for the kidneys."

Marv and Herb walked in. They stopped short, seeing Jack at the table.

"Hello, boys," Dad said. "There's time for one game then I'm closing up."

Marv was a great blusher—but he blushed with anger and insult, not embarrassment. A man like him doesn't get embarrassed and is angry and insulted most of the time. I knew what the coloring-up of his face meant— and so did Jack, who gave a sideways look at him then rolled another ball into a pocket.

"You got a table for white folks here?" Marv said.

Dad did a little double take, trying to make things comic. It didn't work. So he said, "All tables the same. She's set up for snooker down the end. Two shillings each."

Marv looked at Jack. "Oughter get a discount."

"Aw, Marv," Herb said. He was always saying that. He put two coins in Dad's hand. "Come on. I'll break."

They took cues from the rack and Herb broke up the balls, and Marv, still sending looks at Jack from his pale blue eyes—mad sort of eyes—lined up his shot. He leaned across the table, potting for a red in the corner pocket, but he miscued—oh it was deliberate—and the cue ball jumped the cushion and rolled across the floor to Jack's feet.

"Well, shoot!" Marv said. "I guess I need some more chalk." Then casually to Jack, "Pick that up, boy."

I thought he meant me. I was the only boy there. I bent to pick the ball up.

"Not you. The nigra."

"Aw, Marv."

Jack didn't move. Well, he did take one short step back from the table. His eyes were very watchful and I saw he wasn't scared but was confused. Marv would not make him pick up the ball. On the other hand he didn't want to fight, not with me there.

Everybody had forgotten Dad. But it never does to overlook him. He might have been fat and comical but in certain situations Dad was proficient. He stepped across and picked up the ball. He put it on the Ozark boys' table, then reached underneath to a little ledge and came up with the butt end of a cue, a two-foot length. A cut-down cue makes a deadly club. Dad smiled. "No fighting, boys." He tapped the club casually on the back of his hand, meaning that's where he would whack Marv if he tried anything.

Marv went redder. His eyes seemed to go a paler shade. Marv was a sort of Viking, a berserker, and he was, I think, close to letting go.

"You get him out."

"We don't have any color bar," Dad said. "You want me to call the MPs?"

"Alf," Jack said, "it's okay. Me and Rex are going." He moved to the door. "Come on, Rex." If he hadn't left there would have been a fight. There's no stopping men like Marv when their blood is up. Jack knew them well and knew that Dad would get into the fight and get himself hurt. He steered me out the door and through the shop, into the street.

"You could have beaten him," I said.

"Maybe."

"You weren't scared."

"Can't let yourself be scared of men like Marv. I been standin' up to them all my life." He grinned at me. "Your daddy, he's a tiger. But I didn' want him in no fight."

"Dad was great."

"Yeah, he's okay. You're a lucky boy." We walked along. "Men like that," he gestured back at the poolroom, meaning Marv, "killed my daddy." He saw my look of fright and disbelief. "A mob of them, they chase him in an alley. An' Daddy, he can't climb that wall in time. They pull him down and kick him."

I waited, but that little bit was all of it. "He was dead?"

"He's dead."

"But—why?"

"Black man, Rex. You heard ole Marv. They killin' lots of niggers 'bout that time."

"They can't do that."

Jack laughed. He should have been angry but I amused him too much. He laughed happily.

"If anyone did that to my father . . . I'd . . . I'd get a gun and I'd go after them and I wouldn't stop . . ."

"Yeah," Jack said, "too right." He'd picked up that bit of slang from us. "I wasn't that big, Rex." He measured with his hands again. "Not so big as a rat."

"The police—"

"Yeah, yeah," he said, "the police. Hey, let's ride this thing instead of pushin'." He straddled the back fender of my bike. I climbed on, he kicked us along, and that's how we arrived home, wobbling up Barrington Road, laughing our heads off.

Mom gave us ground meat and dumplings for supper. And lots of silver beet and mashed potatoes. And sago pudding.

I dreamed that night of mobs and Marvs and rats as big as dogs, and Jack standing up to them and other times running away.

I stood by his side.

I ran away too.

10

The Festival

Our fall festival raised money for the war effort. Jack and Grandpa got the amphibian running and Grandpa sold threepenny rides around the football field. He wasn't ready to try it on the water; there were too many leaks. But *chuggity-chug*, round and round the wheeled dinghy went, with Grandpa at the wheel in a borrowed sailor's jacket and braided hat.

I could drive the amphib. Grandpa had let me have a turn in the paddock by the garden, with Jack as copilot. He wouldn't let me drive it at the festival. I had other duties anyway.

Dawn was there, working in Grandma's vegetable booth. But what Mrs. Stewart gave with one hand she had to take back with the other. Dawn was so happy to be going. She was out in the cowshed as the sun came up, whistling as she milked into her bucket and singing songs as she hosed the yard. So Mrs. Stewart made her unhappy. (Perhaps she didn't do it deliberately; it was just a habit with her to put a damper on happiness.) She looked in the two urns on the tray of the truck.

"Give me that hose."

Dawn made a small shake of her head.

"Come on. Give."

Dawn handed up the hose. Mrs. Stewart plunged it in an urn.

"Turn it up."

Dawn obeyed.

"Harder. And don't you look at me all big-eyed. They ruined my husband in their war. They left me on a farm that'll hardly grow gorse, with a mortgage the size of Mount Cook around my neck. Twenty years—and Rose— and you. Stop looking at me!" She pulled out the hose and thrust it into the second urn. "Well now they can have water in their milk. They wouldn't know the difference anyway. Turn it on harder."

Jack and I stood on the porch and watched Dawn coming up the street. We wondered why she looked so hang-dog. She gave a little grin as she found the candy bar he'd left in the milk pail, but it only lasted a second. I went down and brought the pail back.

Jack had taken his place at the table. Gloria was jitterbugging to radio music by the settee. I didn't like the way her skirt flew out and showed her bloomers. Mom brought a pot from the stove.

"Oatmeal," Jack said.

"Porridge," Gloria cried, correcting him.

"Yeah, porridge." He watched her dance. "Loosen them hips. Hey, now you've got it."

I brought a jug to the table.

"And real milk," Jack said.

Dad came in with his racing form. He looked in the jug. "Real water, if you ask me. She's going to get caught."

"Look who's talking," Gloria said.

"I don't cheat," Dad said huffily. He saw Mom bending at the stove and whacked her behind with his folded racing form. He pulled her away and did some jive steps.

"Cold hands, Alf."

"I'll warm them up." He held his hands in front of the stove.

Jack put milk and sugar on his porridge and took a spoonful. "It tastes okay to me."

"That's because you've got so much sugar." Dad was bothered by a memory. "Into thin air, two whole sacks. Vanished. Poof!"

"Don't look at me," Jack said.

"It wasn't George. I asked him."

Jack wanted to get away from that subject. He asked Mom how her poem was getting on.

"Finished," she said. "Handed in."

"You'll win, Mom," Gloria said, sitting down.

"As long as it rhymes," Dad said. He looked at his plate. "Podge, stodge."

Mom put her hands on his shoulders and pushed him into his chair. "Seat, eat."

Jack laughed. He was at home with us now. I went into the bedroom and came back with his Purple Heart pinned on my shirt. Later in the morning when Gloria asked for something to wear, he fitted his cap on her head at a jaunty angle. Dressed like that, with Mom in her gypsy costume, we got in the hearse after lunch and drove to the festival.

There were booths and raffles and games and contests and running races, a tug of war, a greasy pig, hoop-las, a shooting range, a tea tent where, at a table, Gypsy Nell studied tea leaves in people's cups and told them how lucky they would be. Gypsy Nell was Mom. She wore a scarf round her head and brass curtain rings as earrings and had her eyebrows darkened with soot. "Crossa my palm with seelver," she quavered in a fake Italian voice.

Over at the edge of the parking field, Dad had a radio wired to the battery of the hearse. Jack had helped him set it up. Dad wasn't going to miss the races. He sold beer to selected customers. Dad was in business for himself. We kept away from him that afternoon, pretending he had nothing to do with us.

Grandma had every sort of vegetable in her booth. Her motorcycle stood beside it with the sidecar overflowing with extra stock. Dawn weighed out beans, tomatoes, kumara, pumpkin halves, on her scales. Stipan Yukich, in a dark suit too small for him and a tightly knotted tie, bought her largest pumpkin and carried it around under his arm for the rest of the day.

He eyed Grandma's parsnip wine uneasily. "You put me out of business."

Grandma blushed. "Take a bottle free."

"No, no, I have some left in the last bottle. And thank you for the worms. I eat them fry with batter." He kept his face straight and Grandma didn't decide to laugh until he'd gone away.

Matty was in his best clothes. Every time he spotted Gloria he whipped out his comb and slicked his hair.

Who else was there? Mr. Dent, conducting the town band. Miss Betts, painted up, glamorous, but speaking like a teacher whenever she came across someone from school. Herb and Marv were there. They soon learned where the beer was. Once, when Bob Davies walked by two car rows away, they had to hide with Dad in the macrocarpa hedge. Marv didn't like hiding from a Maori cop.

Jack and I teamed up with Leo. Jack sat between us on the greasy pole and we belted him with sacks filled with straw. He had to turn half around to get at me but soon knocked me off with a couple of swipes. Then he and Leo fought, and Leo's arm worked so fast Jack couldn't get a hit in. Leo's sack thumped him everywhere, ribs and arms and head and face, and Jack tumbled down and lay beside me on the bed of hay under the pole, looking up at Leo with a half-scared expression. Leo raised his arms in victory. He seemed half drunk with hitting. The straw dust spun about him like golden gnats. In things requiring speed, balance, toughness, dexterity, no one could beat Leo, not even Jack.

Later on Leo and I won the three-legged race — and Leo won his age group sprint by a dozen yards. We bought toffee apples and went across to watch the amphibian rides. Grandpa was doing great business. People reckoned the amphibian was better than Bob Semple's tank. Four at a time could ride in it and children could sit at the back and work the tiller, pretending to steer. Up front we'd set my BB gun on a tripod, but that came off early in the day and Grandpa put it out of harm's way in what he liked to call "the bilges."

We decided not to have a ride. We could ride in the amphib when we liked. Most of the children from our class went around. So did Mr. Dent. So did Bob Davies. Next in line were Matty and Gloria. Gloria stood on the box Grandpa used as a step, and Matty, being gallant, vaulted in and held out his hand to help her up. Marv and Herb were next in line. Marv saw his chance with Gloria. He stepped up close behind her, put his hands on her waist and lifted her easily into her seat.

"There you are, little lady."

I had a quick look at Jack. He didn't like it. The Pascoes were his family. Matty didn't like it either but there was nothing he could do. But Gloria, although she blushed, didn't mind. Marv and Herb climbed in and the amphibian sank inches under their weight. Grandpa started off. He went across the field and started back. Marv was talk-

ing with Gloria. When they came close to the waiting
crowd, he saw Jack. His head made a bull-like butt and his
shoulders swelled. The amphibian turned and came along
the front of the crowd. As it went past us Marv reached
down and grabbed my BB gun. He stood up, straddle-
legged, and aimed at Jack.

"Blam! Blam!"

I felt Jack jerk. His chest hollowed and his arms hooked
round. His head dived for cover in his shoulders. I saw a
roll of white in his eyes and white teeth flashing in his
mouth. His lips set rigidly, squared off. He looked as if
bullets had gone through him.

"Jack?"

Marv saw what he had done. He gave a shout of laughter. "Boy, you're dead."

Jack opened his eyes. He blinked. He straightened up.
But somehow he was smaller than before.

"Are you all right, Jack?"

"Yeah, I'm okay. Let's get out."

We went back through the crowd, past Stipan Yukich
holding his pumpkin and looking from his great height at
Marv and Jack and back at Marv again. We walked
through the booths, past Dawn weighing beets, to the tea
tent.

"Have a cup of tea, Jack."

"Yeah, I will. You kids go and enjoy yourselves."

He went in and we heard Mom's Gypsy Nell voice,
"Ah, the talla dark stra-anger."

Jack managed a grin. He went across to her and sat in the customer's chair.

"Gypsy Nell also reads palms."

"Okay," Jack said. We watched while he found a shilling and put it in her hand. Mom opened his palm and traced his lines. "You come from fa-ar land."

"Anyone knows that," Leo said. We went away.

"Can she really tell fortunes?"

"She can a bit. She says so anyway. I don't know." Only the festival made Mom's act respectable.

"Did you see Jack's face?"

"Yes," I said.

"I reckon it's because he's been wounded."

I agreed. I was feeling a little as though I'd been shot myself.

"That Marv's a bastard."

"Jack could beat him." But I wasn't sure any longer. I wanted a hero and Jack would not take that shape.

What did Mom tell him in the tent? Standard things. "You love life."

"Yes, ma'am."

"You love to be happy. You make people happy."

"Well, maybe . . ."

"You must beware of water. Do not travel on the sea."

"That ain't easy."

"I see . . ." What did she see? I asked her later on and she wouldn't say. And I asked Jack. He replied that he didn't know. She'd glimpsed something that she didn't like and she wouldn't tell him what it was. She pretended nothing bad was in his palm and told him easy things like, "You'll be lucky in love." But Mom claimed it was all a game, all hocus-pocus. "Let's forget it."

Leo and I watched the "Test Your Strength" game. Men took off their jackets and flexed their shoulders, spat on their palms. They picked up the mallet and set their legs apart and made gargantuan swings and the slug ran up the groove toward the bell—but never reached it. The tension must have been set very strong. The prize was a cake. It seemed that no one was going to win, and George Perry, roped in to run the game, must have been thinking he'd get off with it himself when the day was over. Then Marv and Herb came along.

"Lemme have a go at that," Marv said.

"The U.S. cavalry has arrived," George said sarcastically.

"Gimme some room."

People stepped back. Marv was a big man and some of his fat was really muscle, I saw. He set his feet wide and worked his soles into the ground. His grunt when he hit was like a tractor starting. The slug whizzed up the groove and it just, only just, reached the bell, which gave a tiny *ding*, lady-like. People cheered. It wasn't enough for Marv.

"Another one. Pay the man, Herb. More room, folks."

He swung the mallet again. This time the bell made a healthy ring.

"Do I win the prize?"

George Perry, looking sour, picked the cake up from the table. But Stipan Yukich pushed through the crowd from the back. He handed Leo the pumpkin, which almost made him buckle at the knees.

"I try," Stipan said. He took his jacket off, draped it on Leo's shoulder, and rolled up his sleeves. The tight little knot of his tie was exactly the shape of his Adam's apple.

"Come on, squareheads!" someone yelled.

Stipan paid. He took the mallet from Marv—after a little tug of war—and set himself in front of the machine. He rubbed his hands on his shirt. The mallet, sledgehammer-heavy for other men, seemed light enough to be made of balsa. Stipan lifted it, felt its balance, gave a nod. He swung it back easily over his head. He made no grunt, but the *whack* of the blow went racketing through the crowd. The slug took off like a weasel. It struck the bell and knocked it off the pole like someone's hat. It dangled, vibrating, on its wire, and the bell itself flew off in an arc and hit the toe of Marv's army boot and dinged again.

Stipan had a huge grin on his face. Leo beamed. We all cheered. Marv trod the broken bell into the ground but no one took any notice of him. Over beyond the stalls the town band started playing the Colonel Bogey March. That stopped me cheering. I turned and wriggled back through the crowd and ran at top speed for the field. I was supposed to be out there, leading my platoon.

I was late. Mr. Dent, marching in front of the band, wagged his finger at me as I ran to take my place. I yelled "Sorry" at him and marched along with the Purple Heart on my chest. We did a circuit of the field and the band marched in twos into the bandstand. They were to play a concert. But first came prizes. I dismissed my platoon and ran to join Leo in the crowd, which broke from behind the ropes and sat on the grass around the stand.

"What'd you think of Dad?"

"He was great."

"We got the cake. See old Marv, eh?"

"Marv's a loony. Where's Jack?" I looked around and saw him coming with Mom and Gloria. We sat on the grass in a group and listened to a speech from our Member of Parliament. He told us the gate receipts and said the prizes would be money and added, "Who knows, some of the winners might even be inclined to put it straight back in this collection box I happen to have. Where is it now? Yes, here it is." I thought that was a cheap trick, but nobody objected. People came up and got their prizes—for jam, for muffins, for scones, for embroidery, for flowers, for vegetables (Grandma won a lot)—and of course it all went straight into the box. At the end came the poetry prize. Mom took off her earrings and her scarf.

"How do I look?"

"You've got soot on your cheek, Mom."

She wet her handkerchief and wiped it off.

"Well, poetry's a gift," said our M.P. "I guess it's beyond us common folk. So friends, we didn't get many entries. In fact, two." There were groans. There were some cheers. "But both, both, of the highest quality. And the winner is . . ."

The trumpeter played *tan-tan-tara*.

". . . Miss Lorna Betts!"

There she was, standing a short way off. She smiled a little smile, gave a little nod as if to say, "Perfectly right." But my poor mom! First she went white. Then she went pink. She caught her breath and I was terrified she'd cry out loud. She was crying inside, I know that. Her poetry made Mom special, in her eyes. In everything else she was happy to be plain Bernice Pascoe. But in poetry she rose to her special place.

Jack put his arm around her and gave a consoling hug.

Miss Betts went up and shook the M.P.'s hand (Dearborn was his name, a little pouter pigeon of a man) and duly dropped her winnings in the box.

"Not so fast. Come back here. Now face the front." He knew she was a teacher and played a game with her, which, oddly enough, made her simper. "Now Miss Betts will read her lovely lines—in a good loud voice." She obeyed; and Mom had to sit through the whole of it. It was, I have to say, much worse than hers. Mom at least had a sense of fun. I can remember the odd line. Here's the end:

> *So, folded in the hills' embrace,*
> *Caressed by warm and swelling sea,*
> *Our town dreams in its one true place,*
> *And this we hope will ever be.*

Dearborn led the clapping. "Ten out of ten," he cried.

"Mine's better than that," Mom said. She was getting angry and that was healthier than being sad.

"'Course it is, Mom."

"'The hills' embrace.'" Gloria made a wide extravagant hug. "She's gone potty."

"Ain't no justice in this world," Jack said.

We got up and walked away and sat under trees at the edge of the park, listening to the band.

"I'll write another one," Mom said. "I'll show them."

"Good on you, Mom."

We listened to the concert and ate some scones Mom had bought in the tea tent. Dawn and Grandma arrived and Matty sat down next to Gloria. After a while Jack reached in the pocket of his pea jacket and brought out a harmonica. He played very softly in time with the band. Leo and his father stopped. Leo sat on the pumpkin.

"I didn't know he could play," Leo said.

"Neither did I."

"I did," Dawn said. "He played it on the launch one day when you weren't there."

That made me jealous. It didn't last. Jack's music was soothing—and later on, throaty, wild, vibrant, wailing, sweet. It made me catch my breath. It made my heart swell until I thought it would leap out through my mouth onto the grass. We had a crowd around us before long. Jack stood up and played with his body swaying. Sometimes he bent forward and sometimes he leaned back, and his hands, cupped over the instrument, imprisoned and let free wonderful sounds. Matty and Gloria started jiving and soon other couples joined in. Some of them could dance very well. The music went out and over the crowd, it looped out like a rope and caught them in. If you'd been high in a tree you would have seen them flowing in to a point, and Jack there like the hub of a wheel.

Over by the hearse, drinking Dad's beer, Marv heard. He switched the radio off.

"My races," Dad complained.

Marv held up his hand to silence him. "Chattanooga Choo-Choo."

Herb climbed on the hood of the hearse and looked over the cars.

"It's the nigra."

The band had finished playing and three bandsmen joined Jack, with drum, accordion, and clarinet. They stood behind him and picked up the tune. Leo and Dawn tried jitterbugging. They did very well. I had no rhythm in me but I stood by Jack, beaming with pride. He was mine, and every bit as good as Buddy Storm.

He slipped his harmonica into his pocket and grinned at Mom and held out his hand. In her gypsy dress, head scarf in her hand, she went flying in, and they danced to the clarinet and drum and accordion. The other dancers fell back to the edge of the circle and Jack and my mother put on a show. At least Jack did. Mom just kept a kind of rhythm and gave him an object to dance around. It was the first real jitterbugging that we'd seen, outside the movies. It was the outside world coming to town. It was the U.S.A. in Kettle Creek.

I didn't see Marv and Herb arrive. No one did. But suddenly Marv's voice came through the music. It was like a
nail grating on tin. "You think that's good. You ain't seen
nothin' yet." With face all red and thick body swollen, he
stepped in. (In defense of Marv, I must say he'd drunk too
much of my dad's beer. Dad, as usual, had to take some
blame.)

Marv grabbed Gloria. He tried to dance but she pulled
away. Matty tried to barge in front of him, and Marv sent
him flying with a swipe. Poor Matty. He went tumbling
across the ring and ended sprawling on the grass between
Mom and Jack, while Marv grabbed Gloria again. I heard
a kind of roar from Stipan Yukich, although I didn't see
where he was. But Jack was quicker. He went across the
circle in three steps. His fingers dug into the muscle of
Marv's arm and he swung him around and back, a huge
heave, and sent him tumbling away, just like Matty, head
first into the musicians, where his jaw made a thump on
the drum. Silence then. You could have heard a voice on
the other side of the park.

Jack speared Marv with his finger. "You keep your
hands off. Boy!"

Marv, on his elbow, took his time. Marv grinned. He
had what he wanted. He stood up. He gave his shoulders
an upward heave, rotated them, loosened them. I've never
seen anyone do it quite like Marv. It made him unhuman,
primitive.

"I'll show you folks how we deal with nigras."

We saw no one else but Jack and Marv. There were only two—Marv taking flat forward steps and Jack circling easily to one side. But someone just as tough and ready was at the festival that day. We'd forgotten him: Bob Davies. I don't know how he got between the two, but there he was, with his helmet straight and a palm the size of a dinner plate thrust in the face of each of them.

"Enough," he said quietly.

"Get out of my way," Marv said.

Bob Davies had been looking more at Jack. Now his head came around. Did he smile or was that more a wolf-twist of his mouth? "I said"—how quiet he was—"enough!" That last word wasn't quiet, though he did not shout. But there was so much weight in his voice it seems to me it could have shifted railroad cars. Marv blinked and took a backward step. Davies's palm closed and his finger pointed.

"You, go that way."

Marv did not move.

"Now!"

Herb scuttled out of the crowd and put himself in front of Marv and pushed him back with two hands on his chest. Davies turned to Jack. His flattened palm still barred him.

"You, that way." He pointed.

"Yessir," Jack said.

Marv, with Herb leaning all his weight on him and moving him one step at a time, said over his shoulder, "You shouldna done that, boy."

"Come on, Jack," Mom said.

They went away. And somehow I stood alone in the circle, it was mine. Before the crowd came swirling across, with chatter and grin, I was alone, and I realized my victory. I had my Jack. I had my Buddy Storm, my Rockfist Rogan.

11

Tiger Coop

I whispered to Dad, "Jack and Marv should have a boxing match."

He smiled at me. Dad had already thought of it. He had the time and place all sorted out. "You keep out of it, Rex. Leave it to me." So I pretended to Jack I didn't know. On Sunday morning I went down to the poolroom with Dad. Marv and Herb were waiting there. Dad opened the seats along the wall and hunted in the junk forgotten there, years of junk.

"I know I put them somewhere. Ah!"

He pulled out two pairs of boxing gloves and held them dangling by their laces. He looked like a hunter with two pairs of ducks—how he beamed. The gloves must have started out brown but were faded to tan and had worn patches like mange. The hitting surface was rough, sand-papery, and the padding had matted so hard you couldn't dent it with your thumb.

"Good enough for Joe Louis," Dad said. He was able to believe what suited him.

Marv chose the pair without knots in their laces. He held out his hands like a professional and Herb slid them on. Then Marv gave a shriek and ripped one off and threw it on the floor. Dad picked it up and shook it and a big spiky weta fell out.

"It bit me," Marv yelled. But I think he only pricked his finger on one of its legs.

"What is it? A scorpion?" Herb said.

"It's only a weta, boys. A cricket. They don't hurt."

Marv was swearing horribly. I reached out to pick the weta up but he pushed me aside and stamped on it with his great wide boot. I'm an entomologist. That's my job today. It was a beautiful weta, very rare. I've never forgiven Marv for squashing it. I said to Dad as we drove home, "I reckon he's yellow. I reckon Jack will wipe the floor with him."

Later in the morning I rode to the vineyard and told Leo about the fight. I didn't tell Dawn. But Jack was at the launch and he mentioned it. Dawn was teaching him to swim. And that morning he gave her lessons on his harmonica.

"I can't do it," she said.

"I can't swim but you're teachin' me. So keep blowin'."

Dawn tried again. Gave up.

"Where will you go when you go to the war?"

"Somewhere in the Islands. I don't know."

"Do you want to fight?"

Jack laughed. "People with guns scare me." He touched his scar. It was no joke.

"Are you scared of fighting that man this afternoon?"

"Nope."

"Do you want to fight him?"

"Nope."

"Why do you then?"

"Well" — Jack spread his hands — "Alf set it up. I guess I gotta go along with it."

"Alf Pascoe is a crook. Everyone knows."

"I can't let him down. They been good to me."

"Huh!" Dawn said.

"I wish it hadn't happened, though." Jack looked sad. "It kinda spoils things."

She got the idea that her job was to protect him.

The match was in a clearing by the river. A line of trees loomed over the scrub on the eastern side, blocking out houses on the hill at the back of town. A dozen acres of scrub with winding paths cut the clearing off from the park. It seemed very safe. No chance of unwanted spectators. No chance of Bob Davies interrupting.

Church bells rang. The good people of Kettle Creek were going to worship. The baddies were at the clearing for the fight.

A single rope on hammered-in posts formed the ring.
Two chairs from our kitchen sat in corners. A keg of beer
was wedged on a table. George Perry was barman. There
weren't enough glasses to go around and the men had to
down their beer and hand unwashed glasses to the next in
line. No one seemed to mind. Dad was going around taking admission money and writing down bets. All the
young tough guys of Kettle Creek were there, some in uniform. All the old tough guys were there too. No children
allowed, but Dad told me I could watch from the scrub.
He didn't mention Leo but I brought him along. As the
fight got nearer we grew bolder. We crept out of the scrub.
We ducked around, catching glimpses of Jack in canvas
shoes and shorts but making sure he didn't see us.

Marv, stripped off, wasn't fat at all. He was built without a waist. He was the same thickness from his shoulders
to his hips. His arms were of an even thickness too, right
down to his wrists, and golden hairs grew all over him,
making him glitter in the sun. Herb helped him on with
his gloves and laced them up. Half a dozen men helped
Jack. It seemed to me they were sorry for him. He looked
only half the weight of Marv.

To keep our spirits up Leo and I crawled into the ring
and started sparring. Some of the men egged us on. They
wanted real punches and some blood. It might have come
to that. Boys who start out sparring often end up punching. But Dad stepped between us suddenly.

"You boys clear out."

"Aw, Dad."

"This is men only. Go on, beat it." He sounded very bossy, but touched my shoulder in apology. "Jack says." I looked through a parting in the crowd and saw Jack watching me. He gave a small shake of his head.

"There's no fight while you're here," Dad said. "I'm sorry, boys."

I was almost in tears. "That's not fair." I would probably have said, "Jack's mine," but Leo tugged me away.

"Come on."

I followed him out of the ring.

"Pretend we're going."

We went into a path, letting Dad see, and Jack see too, but as soon as we'd gone around a bend Leo headed off into the scrub. We crept along a zig-zag route back to the line of trees and chose the one with the thickest foliage. Up we went, forty feet, climbing silently. The whole of the clearing came in view, with the scrub behind it, then the park and half the town.

"Better than a ringside seat," Leo said.

I was sulking. "Too far away." But he was right. We got a better view than anyone.

Marv was in the ring, sitting in the corner farthest from us. Jack got in. He swung his eyes along the line of trees. He must have guessed what we would do. Leo got us back in the leaves in time. Jack sat down and went out of our sight. Then Dad got in. I hadn't known he was referee; but I was proud of the way he strutted. I thought he might help Jack somehow too. I'd seen how lightly built Jack was and my dream of uppercuts and left hooks wouldn't stand up. Jack had the build of a runner, not a fighter. And Marv—Marv was a hippo, a Tony Galento.

Dad wiped his mouth. "Gentlemen," he cried. The talk kept on. "Shut your traps!" That worked better.

"Right. Now. Here goes. This is a heavyweight bout—"

"He's no heavyweight," someone cried, meaning Jack.

"What he lacks in weight he makes up for in skill. Enough interruptions. A heavyweight bout. Betwee-een. On my ri-ight. Batt-ling Mar-vin Var-coe from the O-zark Moun-tains." What a talent Dad had. He got cheers. "He's won all his fights by knockouts, this boy, and listen, gents, he once knocked out Max Schmeling—in one round."

They hooted with derision. They loved it. Marv was on his feet, waving his gloved hands above his head.

"And now—on my left—the one and only Ti-ger Coo-oop from Chi-cago." Jack stood up. He raised one hand, acknowledging the cheers. "What a real champion this boy is. He's sparred with Max Baer and Tommy Farr and he once went ten rounds with the Brown Bomber himself."

Jack shook his head in wonder. There was no way of keeping Dad in check.

Dad called Jack and Marv into the center. He stood between them, tubby, speaking low, while they stared at each other over his head. I don't know what Dad said—the rules I guess, the number of rounds, the purse for the winner (minus expenses)—but at the end he told them to have a good clean fight.

"Can't fight clean with nigras," Marv replied.

I saw how Dad looked anxious. Even for him things might turn ugly in the end and his dream of profits, good sport, admiration, turn into broken ribs and broken noses. I think he saw what he had got Jack into. But what could he do now? He told them to go to their corners and come out fighting when they heard the bell.

The seconds lifted out the chairs. George Perry was timekeeper—and, being George, made everyone wait. He eyed his stopwatch, raised a little handbell, gave a sharp tinkle at last.

Marv sprang out. He was low to the ground. He held his head forward and his arms spread out. He seemed to come rushing straight at me as well as Jack. His gloves seemed to whistle as he swung. Jack hardly had time to get out of his corner. One, two, those gloves went swooping round in huge blows. Jack vanished. I thought for a moment he had gone down. But all he had done was duck under the punches and slip by Marv, and then—it was like magic—Jack appeared in the middle of the ring. Marv had almost thrown himself off his feet with the punches. He staggered as though he'd been hit and took a moment to find Jack again. Then, with head like a ram and fists out front, he rushed again.

Jack sidestepped, flicked his glove, hit Marv's nose. We heard the smack high in the tree. Marv stood still. Then he roared. He located Jack off to one side and ran at him, to wrestle, I think, not to box. Jack bent his knees, halving his height, and hit Marv, right, left, right, in the stomach, on the jaw, on the side of his head—and Marv fell down. We did not hear the blows. Everyone was yelling too loud. I was yelling too. "Come on, Jack! Come on, Rockfist!" Leo grabbed my arm and tugged so hard I almost lost my grip on the branch. I looked where he was pointing. Davies's black car was racing across the park.

"The cops," Leo yelled.

The car came to a halt, skidding half around. Puffs of dry grass rose like smoke under its wheels. Davies jumped out. And from the other door Dawn Stewart came. She waited there. Davies ran into the scrub.

Leo was halfway to the ground. I climbed down after him. I almost dropped down the tree, grabbing branches to slow myself. For once I was faster. I ran ahead of Leo through the scrub and burst into the clearing, wormed into the crowd, fell over the rope into the ring. Marv was on his feet again, with blood on his mouth. He was stepping forward heavily, slow and sure, and Jack was circling. I think Marv would have been too strong in the end. But it never ended, not that way.

"Police!" I yelled. And Leo, behind me, yelled it too.

It was like an ant nest broken. Men went off in every direction, or seemed to go in three ways at once. Several tripped and fell, but were up again and crashing head down into the scrub. One, I heard later, swam across the river in his clothes. Dad took off. He was first. George Perry vanished in a puff of smoke. Herb got Marv, ran him over the fallen rope and half off balance into the scrub. I don't think Marv knew what was happening. I took Jack.

He ripped off his gloves and let them drop as I pulled him along. Leo, thinking fast, very calm, gathered Jack's clothes and got Marv's too and ran with them heaped in his arms.

We got into the scrub and found a place to squat. The clearing was empty. Distant yells sounded by the river. The ring had two posts fallen and ropes drooping from the other two. Our kitchen chairs lay on their backs in the grass with Jack's boxing gloves curled and blood-stained nearby. The keg of beer stood on the table and empty glasses glittered in the sun. That was all Bob Davies found when he came charging into the clearing.

He stopped. He listened. Yells and crashes, moving away. He could have caught someone if he'd tried. He could have found out who owned the chairs. But Davies, in his way, was an idealist. He wanted the perfect arrest. He wanted Alf Pascoe red-handed. Nothing else would do. He'd missed getting him for the sugar and now he'd missed him at the boxing match. Well, he'd wait. The day would come. In the meantime . . .

Davies picked up Jack's gloves and tossed them aside. He pushed a corner post over with his boot. He went to the table and took a glass and wiped it clean with his handkerchief. He ran a glass of beer from the keg and held it up toward the silent scrub. "May the best man win." Then he picked up a chair and put it on its feet. He sat in the sun and drank his beer. We had to wait there squatting in the scrub until he was finished.

12

Flapjacks, Milk, and Lootenant Paretsky

We went back to town a roundabout way and dropped Marv's clothes over the fence into Whalleys' yard.

"It was Dawn who brought the cops."

Jack looked surprised.

"She was in Davies's car," I said. "How'd she know?"

"I told her."

"Why?"

"Why not?"

"She's a rat. You would've knocked him out."

"Maybe I didn't want to, eh?"

Now it was my turn to be surprised.

"Maybe I didn't want any fights in Kettle Creek."

I muttered at that. I couldn't see what he meant. "I'll fix her."

"No, you won't. You don't say nothin'."

"Why not?"

"'Cause I'm tellin' you." He didn't often speak as sharply as that.

"Anyway, you knocked him over," I said.

"Sure. Good punch." He was humoring me. "Right hook's a good punch."

We went to the launch and found Dawn there. I left her alone until Jack went into the wheelhouse to change into his bathing suit. Then I darted at her snakily. "You stopped him winning. He was going to win."

"He didn't want to be in a fight. Your father made him."

"Liar! You wait till he's gone. I'll get you, Stewart."

Jack appeared in the doorway. "Now you listen, all of you." I was mutinous but I obeyed. "You're my buddies, one, two, three. And me makes four."

"Sure," Leo said. He wasn't upset about the fight.

"Okay, Dawn?"

"Yes, okay."

"Rex?"

"She told the cops. We should kick her out."

"Nobody's out. We're buddies."

"And it's my launch," Dawn said.

Jack went into the deckhouse and came back with four apples. He gave one to Leo, one to Dawn.

"Take it," he said to me. I took it but wouldn't bite.

"What happened, that's over," Jack said. "Too nice to quarrel, this sun."

We sat on the deck and ate our apples. Even I ate mine in the end.

"Will you go back to Chicago after the war?" Leo said.

Jack nodded. "That's home."

"The war will go on for years yet," I said crossly. Jack gave me a patient look.

"Do you really have to go tomorrow?" Dawn said.

"'Fraid so."

"Can you come back for a vacation?"

"I'd like that. I sure would."

"Chicago's better than Kettle Creek," I said.

"It's bigger, that's for sure," Jack said. He threw his core away. "Nowhere's better."

"They should let you have a longer vacation."

"Soldiers don't get vacations. He's got to go and help win the war." Everything I said to Dawn was contemptuous.

"What I've go to do is learn to swim. Who's my teacher?"

"Me," Dawn said.

"No, me."

Jack stood up. "I reckon I'll have one on each side." He grinned at Leo. "And one underneath, to stop me sinkin'."

So we spent that last afternoon teaching him and by the end of it he could dog-paddle across the creek, with his head held high. It was his helplessness in the water that calmed me down and made me start behaving in a reasonable way again. I think we all felt the same toward him — protective, and yet somehow protected by him. Equal to him, accepted, yet innocent and simple and silly alongside Jack and all the things he knew.

I lay in bed and watched him pack his bag. Mom had ironed his shirts and he held them to his face.

"Still warm."

"Will you write letters to us?"

"Sure I'll write."

"And tell us where you are?"

"Can't do that. They don't allow that. I'll send you some cigarette wrappers. Rare ones, eh?"

I felt under my pillow and pulled out the Purple Heart.

"Jack."

He took it and dropped it in his bag, never a glance. Then he turned out the light, opened the curtains, got into bed. He tapped a Camel out of his pack and lit up. Just as on that first night, his face came forward from the dark and sank away. The scar turned pink and faded out in time with it. I felt a dull ache in my own shoulder. Perhaps I'd been swimming too hard that afternoon.

"You don't like the war, do you?" I said.

Jack laughed at my way of putting it. "I don't like the chance of gettin' killed."

"We've got to stop the Japs though."

"Yeah, I guess." He drew on his cigarette. His face lit up, then dimmed.

"They won't get you, Jack." I scrambled out of bed and turned on the light. Jack flicked the curtain across. "Blackout," he said.

I opened my drawer and took out the drawing I'd meant to save for him till morning. "I did this for you."

It was my usual crude affair, drawn in side-view. A man, coal black, in boxing shorts and gloves, knocked a white boxer backward through the air with an uppercut. Underneath was printed: KO BY TIGER COOP.

Jack squinted at it. He put his head on one side to see the white man's face. "That's ole Marv." He grinned at me. "Out stone cold."

"Yes," I said, delighted.

"An' this is me? Brown Bomber, eh?"

"Yes."

"That's real good. You draw real good, Rex."

"Will you take it back to the war?" Perhaps I meant it would keep him safe.

"Sure I will." And Jack, just perhaps, understood. He put the drawing carefully in his bag. "Lights out, eh? Got some sleeping to do after all that sun."

As I went to sleep he ground out his cigarette in the ash-tray. But I woke several times in the night and Jack was always awake. Once he was smoking again and once he stood at the window and looked down Barrington Road at our town in the moonlight.

"Can't you sleep, Jack?"

"I'm okay. Jus' thinkin'."

"What about?"

"Lots of things, Rex. Lots of things." He angled his watch to read the time. "It's near two o'clock. You better get some shut-eye."

I raised myself on my elbow and caught a glimpse of moonlit sea, far away. "Are there any Jap subs?"

"Not here. No subs here."

So I went back to sleep. I'm not sure that Jack slept at all that night.

In the morning he cooked flapjacks. Gloria helped while Mom watched from the table and made runs to the stove to make sure there was enough wood on the fire.

"Leave us the recipe, Jack."

"I will. Better turn him, Gloria, he's burnin'." He brought a heaped plate to the table.

"They're delicious," Mom said.

"They're better with maple syrup. That golden syrup ain't no good."

Dad came in with a broken-backed chair. He put it at the table with a flourish. "Presto!"

"I don't want that. I want my own chairs back," Mom said.

"Temporary measures, love. I'll have a six-piece suite for you on the carrier tonight."

"You're lucky he didn't take your beds and sofas," Jack said.

"Ole Marv could've done with some bed rest," Dad said.

We feasted on flapjacks. Then Gloria had to leave for her bus.

"Hey," Jack said, "I don't see you anymore."

"Isn't it sad?" She was only half joking. She threw her

arms around him. "Goodbye, Jack. Thanks for punching
Marv for me."

"Any time."

Gloria grabbed her bag. She walked out fast and jaunty,
but I saw her wipe her eyes as she went by the kitchen window. And soon only Jack and I were left. Dad called Mom
to the bedroom to hunt for a shirt. She'd washed and
ironed Jack's clothes but hadn't got around to his.

"Did he give you some money from the fight?" I asked
Jack.

"I don't want money." He forked another flapjack onto
his plate. "Don't you go till I finish eating."

"No, Jack."

"You eat too."

"I can't . . ." I'd had six already. I was bursting.

"Just one, eh?" He put a flapjack on my plate. "There,
eat."

I obeyed. I saw he didn't want to be alone.

Mom walked down to the 10:20 bus with him. She kissed
him and gave him a bag of fruit and put him on. The bus
went through the main street, where Dad waved from the
barber-shop door, and ground up the hill past the school.
It was morning playtime. Dawn and Leo and I waited by
the fence. The bus, a green and yellow rattletrap with
gears that seemed to lose teeth at every change, went by.
There was Jack, waving at the window, grinning at us. He
looked happy to be going but I knew that was a pretense.
He shifted to the back seat and waved from the rear win-

dow, and that was how we saw the end of him, framed there, smiling, diminishing. The bus turned the corner, leaving its dust.

Leo said, "It was Marv and Herb."

"What?"

"On the bus."

"I didn't see them."

"Nor did I," Dawn said.

"They were there. On the other side."

"Jack's all right. He's not scared of them."

"They can't do anything on the bus," Dawn said. She turned from the fence and walked away. I looked at Leo. It seemed there was nothing to keep us together now.

"Got to go to the outhouse," he said. And went.

I leaned on the fence until the dust at the corner had drifted into the gorse. Then I walked across the playground to a seat by the chestnut tree and sat down and read my *Champion*. But somehow, that day, Rockfist was unreal.

After lunch Miss Betts came in rubbing her hands together. "Instead of nature study we'll have science. Who wants to see an experiment?"

Our hands went up.

"Good. Now, watch carefully because after this is done I want you to describe it in your books. Why do we do experiments? Dawn Stewart?"

Dawn thought. "To find things out?"

"Exactly. We find out, for example, what sort of minerals are in rocks, or what the air is made of, and so on."

"The air's just made of air, Miss Betts," Nancy Barnhill said.

"That's what you think. I'll tell you about air another day. Now—to do experiments we have to have equipment. So . . ." She took three jars from her cupboard and put them on her desk. We laughed.

"They're just jam jars, Miss Betts."

She didn't get upset. She only smiled. "They're containers. They hold liquid. We don't have to be Madame Curie in her lab. I've got a mark on each of them, you see, three-quarter-way up. Who can guess what we're going to test?"

Nobody could. Miss Betts went to her cupboard again. She brought out a bottle of school milk and held it up.

"Milk's just made of milk, Miss Betts," Nancy said.

"Oh indeed. Shall we see?" She shook the bottle and took out the cardboard stopper. "Tell me when I get to the mark."

"Now, Miss Betts."

"Now."

"You've gone over."

Miss Betts smiled and drank a bit from the jar. We'd never seen her in such a good humor. "Now, two more." She took them out, catsup bottles, and held them by their necks like hanged men. "More milk." She put one on the table and screwed the top off the other. "This is McDonalds', fresh this morning. Tell me when." She filled the second jar up to the mark. "Now, that's on my right as I look at it. Your left. With school milk in the middle. And on my left"—she uncapped the second bottle, poured it in—"Stewarts' milk. Enough?"

"Yes, Miss Betts."

I looked at Dawn. She was watchful. Leo was looking at her too.

"Right," Miss Betts said. "So far we've got three lots of milk from different places. Our experiment is going well. Now we take another piece of equipment." She opened a drawer of her desk and took out a glass tube with marks like those of a ruler on its side and a bulb at the bottom. She held it up for us to see.

"Before I tell you what this is, some facts about milk. It's not just milk, as Nancy seems to think. It's all sorts of things. It's got casein; that's what makes it white. It's got fat. That's the part that makes the cream. It's got lactose—I'll write these on the board later on. Lactose is milk sugar, not as sweet as ordinary sugar. It's got mineral salts, calcium especially. That's for your bones and teeth. But—do you know what makes up most of our milk? Anyone?"

No one knew.

"I'll give you a hint. This"—she held up the glass tube—"is called a hydrometer. *Hydro* means . . .?"

I put up my hand. "Something to do with water?" I guess that was a kind of betrayal of Dawn but I couldn't miss the chance of showing off.

"Good. So water is the other important thing in milk. In fact it's eighty-seven percent of milk. That seems a lot but it's quite normal. Now, the second part of the word hydrometer—*meter*—means measure. So a hydrometer is a piece of equipment for measuring how much water is in a liquid. And today we're going to try it out on three different lots of milk, and all of them, you'll see, will come out the same."

She smiled at Dawn. And how—having scored my triumph with *hydro*—how I wished something would happen to save her. She could not even put up her hand to leave the room.

"Let's try school milk first. Watch the little red mark as I put the hydrometer in."

It floated bobbing in the middle jar. Miss Betts looked up to call out the reading, but a car engine sounded in the road. Car engine? Jeep. We were experts in the sound. It stopped at the school gates with a skid of tires. A woman laughed, making a clear and lovely sound. Dawn half stood up.

Leo, in his window seat, had the best view. He turned and looked at Dawn and mouthed, "Your mother." What he could not signal was the driver, the Yank, who jumped out and ran around to the passenger door. He held up his hand to help her down—just like in the pictures, Leo said. Miss Betts flattened craning children with her finger.

"What on earth do you think you're doing? Dawn Stewart, sit down."

Dawn sank into her desk. She sat very still. Before Miss Betts could get busy again, high heels clattered in the corridor outside. That was a sound Miss Betts was expert in.

She put her head on one side. The footsteps came to our door and three knocks sounded, chirpy, rhythmical. Miss Betts gave us a warning look. She crossed to the door and opened it, but not widely enough for my half of the room to see. "Miss Betts?" said a voice. "I'm Rose Stewart. Dawn's mother." Miss Betts did not reply. She turned to us with a frown. "Not a word." She stepped outside and closed the door.

"Your mother. Your mother," everyone whispered at Dawn.

"Bettsy-bum won't let you go," Jim Whittle said.

"I'll go. She can't stop me," Dawn said.

"She's got a Yank," a boy said.

"Her boyfriend," Whittle grinned.

"Shut up, Whittle, or I'll bash you," Leo said.

Miss Betts came back. She closed the door firmly behind her. "Dawn Stewart."

"Yes, Miss Betts?"

"Take your bag. You can have the rest of the afternoon off."

Dawn grabbed her bag and almost ran to the door. We heard a voice outside say, "Dawnie, love," and high heels clatter again; and from the jeep a Yankee laugh. The engine roared and they were off.

"Powder and paint!" Miss Betts said, although she didn't spare them on herself. "Well, what a pity Dawn will miss our experiment. Some of you will have to tell her about it. What we're measuring, children, is the specific gravity of the milk. That means the amount of water in it. School milk. Copy this down." She read the hydrometer. "Eighty-seven percent. Exactly normal. Now, McDonalds'." That read eighty-seven too. "So that confirms it. Now, number three, Stewarts' milk." She put the bulb in and left it bouncing—made it bounce deliberately, I think, to keep her little comedy running longer. It stopped at last. She bent down to desk-top level to read. I saw one eye go huge through the top of the jar. She took her time. Then she rested on straightened arms and looked at the class. She showed all her teeth in a smile.

"How very strange."

Jim Whittle guffawed.

Dawn, meanwhile, was on a picnic. The jeep sped back through town and turned along the beach road. Grandma, on her cycle, with a sack of horse manure from Dunwoodies' farm as a passenger, was enveloped in the dust it left behind, but she made out Rose and Dawn and a pink-faced American with glinting spectacles. She hoped that Dawn would have a happy time.

They came to the beach and spread a blanket and then a tablecloth on top of it. Rose laid out food. Dawn, telling Grandma, mimicked her.

"Look, Dawnie, real ham. Ham in a can. And look at this, goody gumdrops, a pudding in a can."

"Smile, kid. I'm Santa Claus," said Lootenant Paretsky. (Dad should have met him; he was in Supply.)

There was also whiskey in the basket—at least, that is what Dawn thought it was.

"Ooh, Stan." Then Rose said quickly, "Lootenant Paretsky has been fighting in the war so we have to make sure he has a good time."

Dawn thought Rose was beautiful that day. She could not understand how her cheeks had grown so pink and her lips so red and her hair so curly. She did not seem like a mother at all.

Dawn had no bathing suit and so could not swim. Rose and Lootenant Paretsky let their food digest, then changed in the bushes and Rose skipped into the tiny waves and shrieked as though they were ten-foot ones. The lootenant, his pink waist bobbing, chased after her. "They only went in up to their knees," Dawn said.

He chased her in the shallows and round and round she went, shrieking like a girl and keeping just away from his hooked fingers. In the end she let herself be caught— showing, Grandma guessed, some skill in it. (It seemed to me Grandma was sympathetic to Rose.) They fell over in the waves, then sat with the water up to their waists and Paretsky kissed her. Then Rose was up and off again. Paretsky yelled, a little bad-tempered Dawn thought, "Rosie, I'm pooped." Rose let herself be caught again, easily. So it went. Dawn sat cross-legged on the blanket and watched.

I saw them arrive back in town. The jeep stopped close to the barber shop. I'd just got home from school and was leaning my bike on the veranda post. Dawn was in the middle and she climbed out across her mother's knees. I thought I'd never seen anyone prettier than Rose Stewart. She seized Dawn and kissed her. That embarrassed me so I looked at Paretsky and saw him glancing at his watch. He had a smear of lipstick on his cheek.

Dawn got down. "I think we'd better go or I'm going to cry," Rose said.

Paretsky leaned across her and gave Dawn a candy bar. He winked at her. "That's for having such a peach of a mom." The jeep roared. I'm sure he didn't need to roar it so much. It went off spitting gravel.

"Good-bye, love. 'Bye my little Dawnie. Don't tell Grandma we were here."

Away they went, Rose waving. Dawn stood there a moment, her schoolbag trailing from its strap. Then she rubbed her cheek where Rose had kissed her. She turned and came past me. I wanted to stop her and say something kind. I knew how I would feel if my mother were running around with a Yank. But she went by with never a glance. I should have told her about the hydrometer test so that she could have warned her grandma. She was too far down the road when I remembered. I walked a little way and watched her cross the park. Halfway over she found the candy bar in her hand. She swung her arm and sent it flying away. It fell between two small boys playing marbles in the dust. They picked it up and looked at it and ran away fast.

Dawn went home. Later on she went to the launch. It must have been lonely without Jack.

13

AWOL

I was lonely too. I was confused. I could not work out how I'd come to like Jack so much. What were the steps? I knew he wasn't perfect. I knew he was scared of things, scared of Japs. In the water, dog-paddling (trying to), he was worse than a first-grader. But on that first night he was away, I tried reading Rockfist Rogan and Bill Ross, and Jack kept interrupting. His face kept getting in the way. He wasn't fighting Marv or taming dogs or doing jive— nothing like that. He was walking, sitting, talking— grinning at me. I said his name out loud a couple of times when I remembered I wouldn't see him again. As for Rockfist, he was getting unreal. I read a story about striped pajamas his aunt sent him and how his friends tied them on his Spitfire as a joke, and later on Rockfist waved them from the cockpit of a German fighter he'd stolen so his own squadron wouldn't shoot him down. I started feeling too old for that sort of stuff.

"When will Jack's first letter get here?" I asked Mom in the morning.

"Good heavens, not for days. I wouldn't expect him to write too often, Rex, not in the war."

"He promised to write."

"Well, he will. Not yet though."

I went to school. Said nothing to Dawn, though plenty of other kids told her about the hydrometer test. At morning recess I played French cricket with half a dozen boys. Leo joined in. He won the bat and kept it for a long time, but wandered off when he was out.

After lunch I had to drill my platoon. I was tired of it and wished I could resign but knew it wasn't possible in the war. Mr. Dent stood on a chair clicking his teeth and trying to look like Freyberg as we marched by. Miss Betts had gone into town at lunchtime. Although we didn't know it, she went to the police station with the result of her hydrometer test. Bob Davies agreed to pass it on, saying maybe a milk inspector would come, but he refused to act on it himself. Miss Betts should know that sort of thing was no good. How was anyone to know she hadn't put water in the milk herself?

Miss Betts was in a temper when she came back to school. She wheeled her bike through the gate and I didn't see her.

"Platoon," I yelled, "left face!"

They made their usual ragged turn, and ran smack-bang into Miss Betts. She had to let her bike go and jump back. It went down on the asphalt with a crash and her pie shot out of the basket. Someone stepped on it.

"Pascoe!" she shrieked, but luckily for me found a better focus for her rage. "Mr. Dent! Can't you drill your boys better than that? Oh, my pie. That's a ninepenny one. Who's going to pay?"

She strode to the door. "This school is turning into a zoo." Dent hurried after her, digging in his pocket. "Carry on, Pascoe," he managed to say. I put Miss Betts's bike in the bike shed. Then I tried to get the platoon together. They were kicking bits of pie around the playground. "Platoon! Hey, fall in, you jokers." They ignored me. I knew if I didn't make them obey they'd turn me into a joke sergeant major. Then I forgot—forgot the whole thing. A jeep was coming down the hill into town. The two Yanks in it had white helmets and armbands.

"MPs," someone yelled, and we ran to the fence and watched them go by. Two big men. They both chewed gum.

"What do they want?"

"They must be after deserters."

"Did you see their clubs?"

The jeep went out of sight into the main street. I turned from the fence and hunted for Leo. "It must be Jack."

"Who says? They could have come for anything. They might've come for wine."

Sitting through afternoon school was the hardest thing

I've ever done. I listened for the jeep heading back to Auckland and risked looking out the window whenever I heard a car. Miss Betts was in a foul mood. She caught me once and gave me six.

As soon as the bell rang I was out of the room. I was at Dad's shop before most of the others were halfway down the hill.

George Perry was in the chair and Dad was trimming his eyebrows, a tricky job. He did not look up as I burst in.

"Did you see the MPs?"

Dad went snip with a steady hand. "Yep. They came in here."

"What for?"

"You pay attention, Alf, or you'll have my eye out," George said.

Dad stopped cutting and turned to me. "They're looking for Jack."

"What? What for?"

"He's gone AWOL. They've been all over town, son. Bob Davies with 'em."

"At least it keeps Davies off your back," George said.

"Why's he AWOL?"

Dad shook his head. He felt a tiny bit responsible. "It was Marv. He and Jack got in a brawl when they got off the bus in Auckland. Someone called the MPs. Jack took off. And he never turned up in camp so I guess he's running."

"The darkies are noted for long legs," George said.

I glared at him with hatred, and Dad slapped oil on his head and worked it in, shutting him up.

"They've been around to our place, talked with Mom."

"Why do they think he'll come to Kettle Creek?"

"It's the last place he was at. So they think he'll head this way, poor old Jack. There's no place he can hide, though."

"No," I said. But there was a place. I went out and got on my bike and rode away—and already I was cunning. I rode toward home, then went down a side street and crossed the park and got on the road to the estuary. Before long I saw Leo ahead, making his way home at a dogtrot.

"Leo!" I came up fast on my bike. "Jack's run away from camp."

"When?"

"Yesterday. He got in a fight with Marv. The MPs are after him. He's coming here."

Leo's eyes swung to the mangrove swamp. "Does anyone else know about the launch?"

"Only us."

I saw Dawn then, taking a short cut home through a paddock.

"She better come."

"Yeah."

I pushed my bike into the bracken. We climbed the fence and chased after Dawn.

"Jack's run away."

"The MPs are after him."

Like Leo, she looked toward the swamp.

"Who else knows the launch is there?"

"Only Grandma. She never goes."

"Come on." We ran three abreast as far as the mangroves, where Dawn put down her bag and took off her
sandals. Then we walked, not talking, along the edge of
the swamp to the jetty path. We were afraid. We wanted
to find Jack and didn't want to.

Still three abreast, we climbed the fence. The wires
made a squeak at our triple weight. We paused, not
breathing. Down by the dock something splashed.

"Fish," Leo whispered. I tried to believe him. I did not
want it to be Jack. We walked along the planks laid on the
mud and skirted old-man mangroves, jungle trees, and
came to the dock. Dawn pulled at our shirts.

"Me first."

We let her lead. It was her launch. She picked her way
over the rotten boards and put both hands on the launch
rail—swung one leg over, two. Leo followed. I came last.
And there we stood, triangular, waiting for Jack to show
himself. Nothing moved. The tide made little whispers
and sucks in the mangrove trunks.

"Jack?" Dawn said.

No answer.

"He's not here."

"Jack?" She stepped up to the deckhouse and looked in.
Leo and I peered over her shoulders. We would have
seemed a three-headed creature to someone inside. I let my
breath out.

"He's gone somewhere else."

Dawn said nothing. She stepped in, eyes flicking here
and there—cupboards, table, photo, cushion in the cor-

ner. Everything seemed in place to me, nothing was shifted by a single inch.

Dawn knew better. She stepped across to her old patchwork quilt and took the hem two-fingered. She lifted it as though she might uncover something alive. There was Jack's name—Coop, J.E., Pvt—stenciled in faded black on his khaki bag. We heard each other gasp and heard our breathing.

Dawn let the quilt fall into place.

"He did come here."

"Where's he gone?"

"Hiding, I suppose."

I said nothing. I could not work out what it meant. Good or bad? Good and bad? I did not know. It was as if, in a street I walked down every day, something from down below had lifted a manhole cover, and now the hole was there, empty, black; and I waited for whatever might come out.

Leo made a sudden lift of his head. "Listen," he whispered.

For a moment I heard nothing. Then splashing sounded, down the creek. We ran out to the deck. The noise increased. It was like a hippo wallowing. The mangroves parted. Thigh deep in water, Jack appeared, in fatigue trousers and T-shirt. He gave a big wide grin.

"I wasn't sure it was you so I thought I better lie low." He grabbed the stern of the launch and heaved on it to lift himself on board. The deck rocked, making us lurch and shift our feet—and that same lurch went on in my brain.

Then Dawn and Leo ran to him and hauled him over the rail. I didn't move. They hauled him in like a giant fish. He came falling on board, over the rail, with a kind of slither. He lay there a moment, then stood up. He looked very tired. No one spoke.

"Hey, c'mon. It's me, Jack."

"The MPs were here," Leo said.

"I know. I saw them." He grinned. "Kept my head down." He hauled up a bucket of water and washed his legs. He tried to make everything ordinary.

"How did you get here?" Dawn said.

"I walked all night. Slept this morning. I found me a nice barn, full of hay. Then I came down the river this afternoon, kinda sneaky."

"Have you run away?"

He smiled at her but his eyes were shifty. "I had a mite of trouble with ole Marv. He's kinda persistent. He gives me a shove when we get off the bus. So we had a— altercation. Hey, Rex, I'm lickin' him, the old right hook. Then I see the MPs comin', wavin' their clubs, so I lit out. Thought I'd come back to Kettle Creek an' see my buddies."

It was all evasive. It was not in Jack's style. His eyes went slewing at me, dropped away, and come up looking somewhere else.

"You're scared," I said.

"Them's big clubs."

"You're scared of the war."

He stopped pretending. His eyes held mine. His voice lost its phony jump and lilt.

"I never knew a man who wasn't scared of something." He sat down on the engine hatch. He looked at the deck and swept some muddy water with his foot. "Sure I'm scared. I ran away."

Dawn said, "Have you got something to eat, Jack? Have you got dry clothes?" Jack nodded. Then he grinned. "Hey, look't I got." He dug in his pocket and brought out an empty cigarette wrapper—a Philip Morris with a filter tip. "Bet you never seen one of those." He handed it to me. "You'll have to dry it out, it got kinda wet."

I took it and looked at it, and looked at Jack grinning down at me. I crumpled it and threw it away. Then I turned and climbed off the launch and ran along the dock.

"Rex!" Dawn called. I heard the alarm in her voice but didn't stop. I went through the mangroves, climbed the fence, ran up the paddock. The wires squealed again as Leo climbed. "Rex," he called. I ran up the hill toward my bike. His feet were beating closer. He came alongside.

"Stop a minute." He tried to hold my shoulder but I shook myself free. "Wait, Rex." Then he fell back, and made a rush, and brought me down with a tackle. He knelt over me and pinned my shoulders.

"If you bring the MPs they'll put him in prison."

"I don't care." I twisted my head and would not look at him.

"He's not yellow."

I would not look.

"He's been in the war and he got wounded, so what's wrong with him being scared? He wasn't scared of Marv."

"He's scared of Japs."

"You would be too if they came with bayonets."

I tried to buck him off but he put his forearm on my throat.

"He likes us. We're his friends. So we should help him."

I made no answer. Could not think of one. Friendship seemed like something I must swallow. It hurt like the arm across my throat. I did not want friendship if that was it.

Leo let me go. He stood up. "Go on, be a stinkpot if you like. Get the MPs. Me and Dawn are staying with Jack."

He walked away, with swishing feet. I heard him start whistling to show he didn't care. The grass heads leaned over, fringing the sky. My throat ached where his arm had pressed. I felt a tear roll over the ridge of my cheekbone into my hair, cold as a slug. I swallowed and sniffed and wiped my arm across my eyes.

"Friends," I said, and thought it was a stupid ugly word. All the same I couldn't get around it.

After a while I stood up and went back to the launch.

14

Thieving

"What will happen if they catch you?"

"They got a kind of prison. It ain't very nice."

"You'll have to get farther away."

Jack slapped his hands on the rail. "I'll take my chance with *Rose*, if it's okay with you."

"Can you make her go? You could sail up the coast."

"Yeah."

"And find a place to hide."

I sat on the engine hatch and listened, and thought how childish they were, even Jack.

"I could catch me some fish an' trap some rabbits. Rabbit stoo."

"And when it's over come back to Kettle Creek and be a mechanic." Dawn stopped. She realized she'd gone too far

155

ahead. They were quiet for a moment. Jack turned to me.

"What do you think, Rex?"

I did not like all three of them watching me.

"Will she take much fixing?"

"Some. I'll take a look in the engine later on."

"You'll have to find a place to hide your stuff. They'll search the launch."

"You reckon?"

"I bet Bob Davies knows it's here."

"You can't leave your stuff under that quilt," Leo said.

"Down in the engine, eh?"

"They might look there too."

"Under the dock?"

"No," Dawn said. "I know where. Follow me."

She climbed off the launch and led us through the mangroves and turned off at the place where they met the scrub. We went fifty yards down the creek toward the river. Then Dawn stopped and pulled some fern aside. There was Leo's canoe, laid up neatly on a bed of bracken.

Leo turned and gave her a shove.

"Hey," Jack said.

"You stole it," Leo said.

"Yes. I'm sorry."

"My father gave me that." He was furious.

"I would have given it back but I forgot."

"You're a liar, Stewart."

"What's it matter now," I said. "Help me pull it out."

"If it's got any holes . . ." He glared at her. But it had no holes. I saw the good sense of Dawn's idea.

"You can keep it tied by the launch with your gear in it," I told Jack. "If anyone comes you just get in and paddle away. They'll never know. As long as you don't leave cigarette butts and that sort of thing."

Jack turned to Leo. "Okay?" — reminding us that Leo owned the canoe. He might say "ain't no justice" but always treated people fairly himself.

"Yes, okay."

We slid the canoe down through the mangroves. A thin call sounded far away. I thought it was a bird but Dawn straightened up. "Grandma," she said. The call was repeated — "Dawn!" — quite clearly.

"I've got to go. I'll come in the morning." She slipped away. Leo and Jack pushed the canoe into the water. They got in. Leo was taking Jack to the launch.

"I'll see you in the morning as well," I said to Jack. "What about food?"

"I've got enough for tonight."

"Do you need tools?"

"Yeah, could use some. Rex." I had turned away, but turned back as Jack said, "No stealing, eh?"

"Huh!" I said. How did he think I'd get them otherwise? And hadn't he run away from the war? It didn't seem to me he had the right to worry about wrong things I might do.

I found it hard to sleep that night. I'd doze a bit, then some creak in the house or sound outside would jerk me awake and I'd think of Jack on the dark launch, with mosquitoes biting and the cold black water sliding by. Crocodiles were sleeping in the mud. Snakes were coiled on branches in the mangroves. Then I would make myself be reasonable and think of things he would need — matches, candles, a stove, fuel — and the difficulty of getting them would make me resentful. And wouldn't he need gasoline for the launch? And wouldn't the battery be dead if it hadn't been used for so long? All this helped keep other things at bay — but in the end I'd get to them, of course: Jack was scared, Jack had run away. The MPs and Marv were just an excuse. That was one side of my problem. The other: Jack was my friend and I liked him more than anyone I knew and I had to help. All through the night it kept on hurting me like a toothache.

In the dawn I climbed out of bed and got the flour sack I'd hidden in my closet and crept out to the kitchen. It was hard to steal food. Mom didn't take much notice of household things but she'd notice all right if too much was gone. The best idea was to take just a little of lots of things. But what sort of containers would I put them in? You couldn't have loose sugar and loose tea — loose flour and rice. And what about meat? Where would I find some meat for Jack? Stealing wasn't easy.

I put a bottle of coffee essence in the sack, hoping Mom wouldn't notice it was gone. I put in some cheese. Then I got the loaf of bread and the bread knife and cut three inches off. More than that she'd notice. The sound of the knife going back and forth seemed as loud in the kitchen as a log of timber being sawn. When I stopped I heard someone breathing behind me.

I know it's not possible, but my heart turned over. I swung around. King Kong, ghosts, MPs? It was Mom, standing in her nightie, watching me with a frown on her face.

"Mom," I said, leaning on the bench to hold myself up.

She closed the door to the front room and switched on the light. Then she came and took my sack and looked inside.

"And this is for Jack?"

"No—" I began, but she said, "Shush." She took out the jar. "He hates our coffee and chicory. Still, he'll have to put up with it." She put the bottle back and took not the piece of bread I'd cut but the larger piece and put it in.

"Come with me, Rex." She opened the back door and crossed the porch and went into the washhouse.

"Close the door." She shifted a can on a ledge and took a key from under it. She went to Dad's big cupboard behind the door and opened the padlock.

"That's Dad's."

"I know." She opened the door. The cupboard was crammed with goods of every sort, mostly in cans. There was soup and fruit and beans and spaghetti. There was corned beef and Spam. There were Planters peanuts. Everything. And cigarettes too.

"Most of it came from Americans so I guess Jack is entitled to some. Hold the sack." She filled it up but would not put in cigarettes. "You tell him not to smoke. It'll stunt his growth. Is he well?"

"Yes. He's down at—"

"No! Don't tell me." She locked the cupboard. "Now, knife and fork and spoon and plate and mug."

"And can opener."

"Yes indeed." She led me back to the kitchen and put them in and found a piece of string to tie the sack. "Has he got enough blankets?"

"He's got a quilt. Anyway Dawn and Leo . . ." I stopped.

"A great conspirator you are," Mom said. "Now put that under the hedge. And make sure you get away before your father sees."

"Yes."

"Rex." I stopped at the door. "They'll catch him. You know that?"

"No, they won't. Because he's . . ." This time I didn't say too much.

Mom smiled. "Be careful, Rex. Nothing dangerous."

"No. Jack wouldn't let us."

"I know that. You'll be in trouble though."

"If they don't catch him we won't."

I saw she didn't believe he would get away. All she said was, "Give him my love."

There was no time for that. There was only time to run across the paddocks and through the mangroves and hand the sack to Jack and head for school. He was shaving. The lather made his skin seem darker.

"Hey, what's there?" He tested the weight.

"It's all right. It's black market stuff so it isn't stealing." I left it at that. But in the afternoon, after school, I had to take some tools from Grandpa's workshop, and that piece of stealing bothered me. He was melting tar to plug the holes in the amphibian. I stood around, pretending to help, feeding chunks of tar into the pot bubbling on the burner.

"Are you using this wrench much now, Grandpa?"

"Spanner? Nope. Finished in the engine."

I slipped the spanner into my belt and let my shirt hang out to cover it. Grandpa came and looked in the boiling pot. "Lovely brew."

"How long will the war go on, Grandpa?" I really meant, how long will Jack have to hide?

"Hard to say," Grandpa said. "It looks as if Rommel's on the run. And the Yanks seem to have the Japs stopped now." He meant Guadalcanal, the Solomons, where Jack had been wounded. "It might be too late for my amphib."

"We can use it for fishing."

"Yes, we can." That cheered him up. He poured boiling tar in his pail and went back to work. I slipped a screwdriver into my belt.

"Sorry, Grandpa," I whispered under my breath. "I'll bring them back."

I rode up to the vineyard where Leo was also gathering stuff. He'd got matches and two candles, an old portable stove and some fuel.

"He better not light those at night," I said, "or they'll see and think it's a spy."

"The MPs came up here," Leo said. "They've been looking in farm sheds and huts and things. Davies too."

"They won't find him."

But in fact they had come very close to finding Jack and were coming even closer as we spoke. It happened like this. After leaving Yukichs' the MPs went back down the road to Stewarts' farm. Mrs. Stewart, unfriendly as ever, let them look in her sheds, and told them when they'd finished not to come back. They looked on a neighboring farm, then walked along the paddocks to their jeep parked on the road. The MPs were Riley and Bartz, big, heavy men, gum-chewers both. Davies wasn't getting on well with them—didn't like their offhand way. I guess they didn't think a country cop needed listening to.

Bartz saw the track leading into the mangroves. "What's in there?"

"An old launch. Belongs to the lady on the farm."

"Let's take a look."

Jack heard the wires squeal under the heavy men. He had the cowling off the motor but nothing unscrewed—he had no tools yet. He lifted it back on silently, then looked in the deckhouse to make sure nothing was lying around. He'd been very careful in the morning to get all his gear in the canoe. It was just as well. Davies and the MPs were walking through the mangroves. He heard their boots clump on the boards.

Jack lowered himself into the canoe, untied the rope, and paddled away, using his hands. He was only just out of sight down the creek when the MPs climbed on the dock. Jack ran the nose of the canoe into the trees. He looped the rope around a branch and climbed out carefully. He crept back through the mangroves and crouched waist-deep in water, watching Bartz and Riley climb on the launch. Riley was swearing at the mud on his boots. That made Jack smile.

When the three men went into the deckhouse he crept closer.

"Who's that?" Riley's voice.

"Local girl," Davies said. Jack guessed it was the photo of Rose. "You might know her," Davies went on. "She knocks around with you jokers." He was a bit sarcastic, Jack thought.

"MPs?"

"Yanks. Her daughter must use this as a hideout."

They found nothing suspicious in the deckhouse. Jack lowered himself down to his mouth in the water as they came out. He realized he'd gotten too close. But they didn't see him. They went along the dock cautiously, not trusting the rotten boards to hold their weight. When he heard the wires squeak again Jack made his way back to the canoe.

It wasn't there. It was twenty yards away in the middle of the creek. The tide, running out, had pulled its stern around, undoing the rope, and tugged it out. Jack tried wading after it. He got in up to his chin again, then lost his nerve. He thought he might dog-paddle as far as the canoe, but how would he get in without capsizing it, and how could he drag it to shore?

He turned back into the mangroves and climbed through them as far as the scrub. Then he ran along the bank until he reached the track. Up in the paddock Riley and Bartz were ambling along like a couple of Jersey bulls enjoying the sun. They stopped and unwrapped gum and put it in their mouths. Davies looked impatient with their slowness but wasn't going to hurry them, Jack saw.

He worked out the line of sight from the MPs to the creek. The mangrove jungle hid the drifting canoe. But when it reached the river it would come into their sight. And even if they didn't see his gear tucked down inside they'd see his army cap perched on the bow.

Jack ran for Leo. He could think of nothing else to do. He kept in a gully until he reached the road, then ran along to the gate. Matty and Stipan were working at the back of the vineyard. Jack saw them on the rise at the end of the vines. He ran down the drive, keeping the shed between him and the men.

"Leo." We heard his soft cry and ran around from the back where our stolen goods were laid out on the grass. He was standing under the vine trellis by the door.

"Jack!"

He made that self-protective crouch again. He was wet and panting and his feet were white with dust from the road.

"Canoe's gone . . . I lost her . . . the MPs are going to see."

We ran back along the road and down the gully and crept round the base of the hill. Up there, facing away from us, Riley and Bartz were sitting in the grass. Their helmets lay beside them like two giant puffballs. Davies hunkered down off to one side.

"Where is it?" Leo said.

"Down the creek."

We went into the mangroves, wriggled through, came to the water. The canoe was turning slowly, feeling the first pull of the river. Leo and I stripped off our shirts and gave them to Jack.

"You wait here."

Quietly we slid into the water. The running tide helped us along. We swam sidestroke to avoid making splashes and came up fast on the canoe. It was turning in a lazy arc toward the river. We kept on glancing at the mangrove wall and in a moment saw we were too late. The canoe would be out from cover, in the MPs' sight, by the time we reached it. There was nothing to do but keep on going and hope they wouldn't get suspicious.

Leo reached it first. He grabbed the stern. The men up the hill were on their feet. I saw one of the MPs take half a dozen steps along the slope for a better view.

Davies shouted, "That your canoe?"

"Yes, mine," Leo shouted back.

Then I saw Jack's cap on the bow. It sat there at an angle and as Leo hung on the stern it seemed to bob cheekily at the MPs. Too late to hide it. I swam along the side of the canoe and grabbed the cap. I fitted it on my head and faced the MPs and saluted.

"Chuck us some candy, Yank."

Leo paddled up close and pushed me under. He grabbed the cap and put it on his own head. I came up in time to hear him shout, "Got any gum?"

We started fighting for the cap, ducking each other, and the canoe drifted away.

"You kids," Davies shouted angrily. He must have hated our begging from the Yanks. "You get that canoe and get out of there."

We scuffled, and sank, and lost the canoe, and swam after it, and fought again.

"Go on, before you drown yourselves."

We obeyed. The MPs seemed to have forgotten the cap. It was normal in those times for children to have American souvenirs. We got on either side of the canoe and hauled ourselves in and paddled to the creek, and Davies and the MPs, after watching us a moment, walked on up the paddock to the road. We heard the jeep start as we got back to the place where Jack was waiting.

"Too close."

"We fooled them though," Leo grinned.

"I'll get you kids in trouble."

"We don't care."

"I do. I better get out of here real soon."

We left him at the launch, tying up the canoe, and fetched our stolen goods from the vineyard. Jack was upset by the amount of stuff and we had a hard time convincing him it was old or just on loan. His near escape had made him thoughtful. He seemed to realize only now how deep in trouble he was. He did not want us in trouble too.

Dawn arrived. She brought milk and apples.

"Can you make the engine go?" she asked Jack.

He lifted the cowling.

"She's a good motor. Chevy '28. The battery's alive—only just. There's fuel in those cans. I guess your grandma forgot she left it there. But I got a problem."

"Yes?"

"Someone's taken a couple of spark plugs out."

15

More Thieving

He took Grandpa's spanner and unscrewed a plug, which he showed to Dawn.

"Won't go unless there's a full set."

"There's two of those in the shed at home."

"Yeah?"

"In a baking powder can. Shall I bring them?"

"We'll get them. Me and Rex," Leo said. The more action there was, the better he liked it.

"No, you won't," Jack said. "You neither," he said to Dawn. "I'll come tonight."

"The dogs will bark."

"No, they won't. They're my friends. You just tell me where to find them."

"On a shelf. In an Edmonds can. I'll draw a map." She and Jack went into the deckhouse.

"I'll bet they will bark though," I said.

Leo grinned at me. I could almost hear his mind go *click-click-click*. "Want to bet?"

He would say no more than that. As well as action Leo liked a bit of mystery. "Take back one of those cans of Spam."

When we left the launch he took me up to the vineyard. He got an old pail from the shed and we squatted in the grass out at the back and opened the Spam. Leo cut it into chunks with his pocketknife.

"Wait here." He slipped into the shed. I went to the door and watched. Stipan and Matty were working in the yard. Whatever Leo was doing, it was risky. I'd just about had enough risks.

"Get out," he whispered angrily at me.

I went back to the pail and ate a piece of Spam. Very nice. I nipped across to the vines and tried a grape but they were sour. Then I looked in through the door again. Leo was halfway along the shed, squatting out of Stipan's sight, filling a wine bottle from a barrel.

I slid away, back to the Spam. I didn't mind pinching from Dad but I wanted nothing to do with pinching from Stipan. He was too big.

Leo came out. The bottle was three-quarters full. "Port," he grinned. He poured it in the pail on top of the Spam. *Glug glug.*

"My dad told me this. Looks good, eh?"

It looked horrible. It looked like sausage meat in beet juice. "Dogs won't eat that."

"You wait and see."

We arranged to meet at dusk by the culvert on the town side of Stewarts' farm. I told my parents I was going out. Dad said jokily, "Got yourself a girlfriend, eh?" I mumbled that I was going to help Grandpa on the amphib. Mom looked at me sadly — because I was lying or because of Jack, I could not tell.

Leo was waiting. He was doing giant swings with the pail, not spilling a drop. I thought it would serve him right if the handle came off. We left my bike hidden and cut across the farm, and suddenly it was not dusk but dark. We walked into thistles and banged into fences, but found our way more easily when we came to the drive. The dust caught light from somewhere and made a ghostly glimmer in the dark. It dampened the sounds of our feet so we were able to approach the farmhouse silently.

A light was on in the cowshed but it flicked off as we got close. Mrs. Stewart crossed the yard, passing through the dim little puddle of light by the kitchen window. She opened the door and was framed there for a moment as she kicked her rubber boots off. What a skinny, tough, man-like figure she was.

The door closed.

Leo and I were crouched at the back of a water trough. My hands were hot and sweaty and I dipped them in to make them cold. The float that shut off the water when the trough was full made a little bong as my knuckles touched it. A chain dragged and rattled on the far side of the shed.

"Jeez, you're a noisy bastard," Leo whispered.

"I'm sorry."

"Come on. Do it soft."

Our eyes were used to the dark now. The stars were glittery. The shed stood out against the river. Leo ran to the corner. He peered around. I looked over his head. The dogs were lying outside their doghouses, in that hopeless way dogs have, with their heads between their paws. We eased back.

"Okay," Leo whispered. He put his hands in the mess of Spam and port wine and drew out a piece. I did the same, shivering at the slimy touch.

"Right."

We leaned around again and lobbed together, aiming for a spot in front of the dogs. One went *woof!* Not loud. He had no time. The smell of meat and wine overcame his instinct to bark. They wolfed down the Spam, and Leo, unafraid, darted around the corner.

"Come on. Quick." He slopped our stew into a cut-down kerosene can that served one of the dogs as a dish. I found the other and held it as he poured. The dog was slurping at it before I could put it on the ground.

"Let's get out before they finish." We ran back to the corner of the shed and watched from there as the dogs emptied the containers and licked them clean. Then they stood looking at us, wagging their tails.

"They'll be out cold in ten minutes," Leo whispered.

"Where do you reckon Jack is?"

"I don't know. Let's hide and watch."

We crossed the drive and wriggled under a fence and found a blackberry patch twenty yards back in the paddock. "This'll do." We settled down to wait.

Jack left the launch half an hour after dark. He reasoned that movements in the house would cover any noises he might make. And if someone was awake and lights were on, he'd have a better chance of not exciting the dogs. He need not have worried about that.

Jack was afraid of the dark. He'd never been afraid in the city, but out here, with all those empty paddocks, the mangrove swamps, the silent water, and no one to talk to, no voices in other rooms, no cars, no shouts, no laughter outside, he began to imagine ghostly things were creeping up on him. For this reason too he set off early. He wanted to get back inside the deckhouse and close the door.

He came through the paddocks soundlessly. When fences blocked him he'd find a firm post and put his hand on top and vault over as easily as stepping off a curb. The kitchen light was a beacon. When he reached the cowshed he stopped and listened for the dogs. He meant to spend a moment or two persuading them that they need not bark. And they would be company for a while.

He crept along the side of the shed. A strange noise stopped him. He thought it was the croaking of frogs. There had been frogs in the Solomons. He didn't like the sound. Jack crept closer. No, he thought, it wasn't frogs, it was someone breathing heavily. He looked round the corner. The dogs lay in drunken sleep outside their kennels. They wheezed and snored and sighed and licked their chops, dreaming of food, and made no sign of waking as Jack approached.

"Hey boy, hey boy," he whispered. He touched their heads, then wrinkled his nose. Jack knew a drunk when he smelled one. He picked up the dishes and sniffed them — and, he said, worked it out pretty quick. He peered around in the dark, knowing Leo and I would be somewhere close. Then he made up his mind to get the spark plugs and move out fast. His aim now was to get away from Kettle Creek and not land us in trouble.

Dawn was having a nervous time in the house. She was doing homework at the kitchen table while her grandmother sat opposite, working on farm accounts. She seemed confused by them and Dawn felt sorry for her. Being guilty about the spark plugs and the launch did not help. The only sound was the scratching of pencils. Everything was silent outside. Any little disturbance would be heard.

"Shall I make us a cup of tea?" She wanted to make some noise and activity in the house but wanted to do something for her grandmother too.

"It's rationed, miss. Drink water." Mrs. Stewart looked back at her figures. They seemed to puzzle her. It was as if something in her brain had stopped working and the numbers on the paper didn't have a meaning anymore.

"Have you got an eraser?"

Dawn handed it over. "Would you like me to help?"

"I can add. I went to school." But Dawn's offer pleased her and she smiled. "Time you were in bed."

"Yes, soon."

"Cleaned your teeth?"

"Not yet."

"Well, it's late. Better do it now."

Dawn stood up. Then she froze. A faint tinny sound came from outside.

We saw Jack come around the side of the storage shed.

"There."

"He must have found the dogs. Sloshed, eh?" Leo grinned.

I didn't like the light from the kitchen window. It touched Jack and made his eyes gleam.

"She should have her blackout curtain closed. We should report her."

"In he goes."

Jack had reached the shed door. He opened it without a sound and went inside. A little flare of soft light showed before a hand came back and shut the door.

"He's struck a match."

"He's got to see."

I tried imagining the inside of the shed: junk piled high, narrow paths between.

"Dawn should have put them near the door."

"He'll be okay. Hey! Ssh." We heard a faint sound—Jack's foot striking an empty can. Our eyes swung to the house. Mrs. Stewart appeared in the kitchen window. The frame squeaked as she pushed it up. She put her head into the night and peered around. It must have puzzled her that the dogs were not barking.

"Dave! Dot!" she called. The dogs were silent.

"Dave!"

She would probably have come outside to investigate and not thought of looking in the shed. But a sound—a clatter, a crash, a bucket symphony—came from in there. Mrs. Stewart sprang back from the window, disappeared.

Jack's match went out as he saw the baking powder can. He risked a step in the dark and reached for it. That is when the toe of his shoe hit an empty can—the first of the sounds. But he had the can, and twisted off the top, and felt the two spark plugs inside. Then he heard the kitchen window squeak and he stood very still. Mrs. Stewart called the dogs. That alarmed Jack. He knew she would come outside to see what was wrong and it seemed to him she would surely look in the shed. He had to get out of there fast and get far away. He took a step, then realized he would have to strike a match to find the door.

As he fumbled with the matchbook his elbow nudged something—he never knew what—and that began a domino collapse. Things came down from everywhere. The shed was like a room with a jazz band playing, Jack said. He lost the matches but held on to the Edmonds can and managed to work his way to the door. That was as far as he got.

We saw Mrs. Stewart leave the window, saw Dawn look out, then chase after her. The back door opened and Mrs. Stewart stood on the step.

"Who's there?" She reached sideways and picked up a walking stick that must have been leaning on the wall by the door. It had a heavy knob instead of a curved handle.

"You'd better come out. I've got a gun."

Liar! I wanted to yell. She came down the steps and Dawn appeared in the doorway. "Grandma," she cried.

"Go back inside."

"She's going to find him," I said to Leo.

"No, she's not." He stood up. He still had the pail in his hand and he sent it sailing with an easy heave into the yard. It bounced and clattered across Mrs. Stewart's path. She swung around.

"Hey, Ma Stewart," Leo called.

I got the idea and jumped up. "What do you put water in your milk for, Ma Stewart?"

We were too far back in the dark for her to see but she must have caught the flash of our faces.

"Who are you?" She ran at us, and stopped, and ran again.

"Over here. You're blind."

"Why don't you wake your dogs up?"

"Why don't you shoot your gun, ha ha!"

So we led her away, keeping too far ahead for her to make out who we were. And Dawn ran down the steps and crossed the yard. We saw her open the door, saw Jack come out and talk with her a moment and slip away into the dark.

Then Dawn stood in the yard and called, "Grandma. Grandma, come back."

We ran then and easily got away. We reached the road, got the bike, went our different ways. We were very proud of ourselves. If it hadn't been for us Jack would have been caught.

But today I'm not pleased with it anymore. Mrs. Stewart had too many troubles and was close to her breaking point. We upset her very badly that night and we have to take our share of blame for the things that happened after that.

16

Gifts

Jack was angry with us when we went down to the launch in the morning. Better he got caught, he said, than we upset an old lady like that.

He was working on the engine. The thing he wanted most was to get away up the coast. Then if he was caught none of us would get dragged in. He meant to get the engine going in the next two days, or ready to go, and he told us not to come after school because he'd be busy. This, we realized, was his way of keeping us out of trouble.

"Can we come tomorrow, Jack?"

"Yeah. Early, eh. So no one sees. You tell Dawn."

But Dawn was not at school. We didn't see her until the following morning, the Saturday, at the launch. She'd been there half an hour when we arrived. By this time we had a signal, a shout broken into bits by a hand on the mouth, wa-wa-wa, to let Jack know it was only us.

He was eating cold beans from a can when he heard Dawn. He made a soft clear whistle in reply. A moment later she stepped along the dock and climbed on board. He had not seen her since their brief meeting at the shed. Now he sensed a kind of hurt in her.

Softly he said, "How's your grandma?"

"She stays up all night. She won't talk. She talks to herself. She's got my grandpa's old shotgun out."

He did not know what to say. He got a spoon and offered her some beans.

"No," she said.

"The dogs all right?"

"They woke up. Rex and Leo shouldn't have done that."

"It's my fault."

"No, it isn't. Anyway, do the spark plugs work?"

He showed her the engine with the plugs in place. "I think she'll go. Can't try it out in case someone hears. I just got a few things left to check. Rudder and propeller and so on. But it looks okay."

"I drew a map." She took it from her shirt and opened it out on the deck. They knelt and studied it.

"You go out through the bar. It's safe at high tide. Then you go up here, as far as this headland. It's got big yellow cliffs, so you can see. There's creeks and bush on the other side. You can go right up the creeks and anchor there."

"Thanks, Dawn. I won't get lost now." He tried a joke. "Can't find Chicago on that big map at school but I guess I can find me a little creek. Hey, Dawn, I got something for you."

He went into the deckhouse and came out with his harmonica. Dawn was overwhelmed.

"I can't play," she whispered.

"You'll learn."

"I'll practice. I promise I will."

"When I come back I want to hear 'Chattanooga Choo-Choo.'"

Leo and I signaled from the fence. Dawn put the harmonica in her shirt. She went into the deckhouse and started straightening up, although there was little that needed doing. Jack still kept his gear in the canoe, which was tied alongside.

We came on board. Leo had a bottle in his hand.

"What's that, gas?" Jack joked.

"It's wine. For you." For once he was shy. "It's some of Dad's best."

"I'm surprised you got any left." That was a reference to our escapade of two nights before. It reminded Dawn of what we had done. She came bursting out of the deckhouse.

"You leave our dogs alone."

"Okay," we said.

"I don't like my grandma being upset."

"It worked."

"She would've caught Jack if we hadn't yelled," Leo said.

"You stay off our farm from now on."

"Who wants to go on your moldy farm?"

"Hey, hey," Jack said. He calmed us down and thanked Leo for the wine. Dawn moved to the rail. She touched her shirt. "Thanks, Jack."

"Wait up, don't go."

"I've got some jobs for Grandma."

"I'll show them your map first, eh?" He was trying to bind us together. We knelt on the deck and looked at the map.

"Not bad," I said to Dawn. In fact it was very good. She had everything marked and everything in scale. The bar was there, the reefs were there, the creeks and hills and bush were there. I had not realized she knew the coast so well.

"This is the dangerous part. There's houses here," Leo said.

"Will you go tonight?"

"Yes."

"You'll have to sail blind. They'll think you're the Japs if they see any lights."

"Can we come down and see you go?" I asked.

"No." Jack swallowed. "Fact is, I don't want you coming down again."

We protested. Dawn joined in. But Jack had made up his mind. "It's too dangerous. You kids done too much already. You'll be in real trouble if they catch you." He would not be swayed. We stood and looked at him, knowing that when we left we would never see him again. This was good-bye. There had been no time to get ready. It was like getting a bad fright. My stomach seemed to shrink to the size of a green apple.

Dawn went first. She put her leg over the rail. Again she touched her shirt. " 'Chattanooga Choo-Choo.' I promise." A comment that Leo and I could not understand.

"Sure," Jack said. "I'll come back ridin' on it, you wait and see."

She went onto the dock.

"Dawn."

She turned.

"Keep on smilin' that old smile."

She gave a small nod. Then she was gone into the mangroves. We stood silent.

Leo moved. "I've got to go too."

"Here," Jack said. He slipped out of his pea jacket and fitted it on Leo's shoulders.

"For me?" Leo was delighted.

"Yup, for you."

"It's still warm from your arms. Won't you need it?"

"I've got a spare one."

I was jealous. "It's too big."

"He'll grow. If you grow as big as your daddy," he said to Leo, "it won't last long."

"I'll always keep it."

Jack shook hands with him. "I'll leave the canoe. She'll be tied up at the dock here. So long, Leo. Without you kids, without my mates, eh, I get caught."

Leo climbed the rail, went surefooted along the dock

into the trees. That left me. All this time I'd been holding a gift for Jack in my hand. Now I gave it.

"I brought you something to read."

Jack untied the string and let the paper open out. He smiled with pleasure. He knew how important the *Champion* was to me.

"Rockfist Rogan. Hey, thanks. I've still got your drawing."

"Good," I said. I turned to leave.

"Wait up, Rex."

He felt in his shirt pocket. Pulled out the Purple Heart. Jack had worked out his gifts carefully.

"You keep this."

"No . . ."

He took my hand and put the medal in.

"I don't need it anymore."

But I could not close my hand on it. It seemed too important, and seemed to mark an ending too much.

"Kettle Creek's the best thing that ever happened to me," Jack said.

So I took it. My fingers closed. I opened my mouth to speak, but could not speak. All I could do was nod my head once, as Dawn had done.

I climbed the rail, walked on the rotten dock for the last time, went into the mangroves. I looked back from there and raised my hand, and Jack raised his and grinned at me. Then I went on and Jack was gone.

17

Meanwhile . . .

The last part is very hard to write. I think about it often these days, and think that if I'd behaved sensibly, not gone to Stewarts' farm that night, shown Jack sooner that I liked him, then it would have ended the way we planned, Jack would have sailed out on the tide, over the bar, and got away. But that's unreal. You can't change the past. And it didn't just depend on me anyway. All sorts of people got mixed up in the story of Jackson Coop.

For that reason, too, it's hard to write. Everything went crazy on that day. People were running everywhere, doing this and that, and then it all came to a point and Jack was the focus of it all.

I'll start with Grandma. She was out collecting cow dung that morning. Although she was old, she had sharp eyes. She saw Dawn far away, walking in the paddock. Then she saw Leo climb the fence and run up the hill the other way. It made her suspicious. Why had they been meeting? They were much too young to be in love. Then she saw me. I climbed the fence and walked along looking at something in my hand. She saw it gleam.

Grandma climbed high up the hill, where few people went. From there she could see the creek as well as the river. The launch roof showed in the mangroves and soon she saw someone moving there. She could not tell who it was but she could guess.

Grandma went home. She emptied her wheelbarrow (no matter what happened, her garden came first), then put on her motorcycling gear and rode to our place. Only Mom was home.

Mom, sitting at the kitchen table writing another poem:

> *Run, run, poor black man,*
> *Where can you hide?*
> *Cruel men with guns*
> *Close in on every side.*

"Listen," she said as Grandma walked in; and she read it, all sixty lines. Grandma listened politely.

"Yes, Ber, very good," she lied. "But you don't have to ask where he can hide. He's found a place."

"Where?"

"That old launch of Joan Stewart's."

"Ah. I wondered."

"So you knew?"

"I knew he was somewhere in Kettle Creek."

"And Rex is helping him?"

"Yes."

"And Dawn Stewart and Leo Yukich?"

"Yes, I knew they were in it."

"Don't you think it's too big a responsibility for them?"

"I suppose it is."

"Well, come on then."

"Where?"

"Let's go and see him, Ber. Let's find out what it's all about."

By that time I was at the barber shop. I saw them go by, Mom in the sidecar, hair tied up in her gypsy scarf, and Grandma with wild hair and goggled eyes. I thought nothing of it; I supposed they were going to Grandma's place, and I turned inside to see what job Dad had for me next. They rode on and left the motorcycle parked at the side of the road and walked down the gully to the mangrove swamp.

Jack was waist-deep in water. He was scooping buckets of mud from around the launch's keel, making sure it would free itself easily that night—and he didn't like the feel of the hull down there. He tried it with his fingers, pushing into crevasses of rot. They didn't go right through; but would the rotten places hold when the launch got out into the waves?

He looked up and saw two grave faces watching him.

"Ladies," he said calmly. "Climb on board. Easy does it, though. She's likely to sink."

He hauled himself out of the water and pulled them onto the launch, one by one. They sat on the deck and he told them all that had happened and what he planned to do.

"I guess now I'm running I got to keep running. Guess I'll hide a while. But I got to come out in the end. Then . . ."

He did not go on but Mom and Grandma knew what he meant. How can a black man hide in a country where most people are white and the rest are brown?

"We can give you the names of some people who might help," Mom said.

"No," Jack said. Then, more softly, "No, ma'am. I'm not getting anyone in trouble. Already I got Rex and Dawn in trouble."

"It's doing Rex good," Mom said.

"Maybe." He looked at Grandma. "You do something for me?"

"If I can."

"Dawn's grandmammy don't seem too well. Not her fault. Part my fault. But I think Dawn needs someone lookin' out for her."

"Yes, I know," Grandma said. "I'll call in when you've gone. I'll watch her."

"Thank you, ma'am."

"When will you go?" Mum asked.

"Tonight."

"Watch the bar."

"It's high tide. Dawn made me a map."

"How far can you get?"

"Don't know. Not far. I thought I had two cans of fuel but one's no good, got condensation in it."

Mom and Grandma looked at each other. They were like that at times, almost telepathic. Both had the same idea at once.

Dawn was in more trouble. When she came up to the farm after leaving Jack, she hosed out the cowshed, which hadn't been done after morning milking. In fact they'd barely got the shed work done that morning—sent cows out half milked—and Mrs. Stewart had topped up the urns until water ran over their rims. And out on delivery they'd missed a couple of streets—Mrs. Stewart said she couldn't care less—and came back with one of the urns still a quarter full. It was sitting on the back of the truck. Dawn wondered if she should empty it. Instead she looked at the dogs, patted them, and fondled them. They were all right again after their wine party, but they needed exercise and she wanted to let them off their chains.

She went inside. Mrs. Stewart was sitting at the table.

"Where have you been?"

"Hosing the shed. Can I let the dogs loose?"

"No."

"Grandma—"

"I want them here, not running around. In case those boys come back."

"They won't come."

"If it's not them it'll be someone else. They're never going to leave us alone."

"Grandma, get some sleep. You didn't go to bed at all last night. I'll do the jobs."

Instead of replying Mrs. Stewart gave Dawn a long, bitter look. She reached into her pocket and drew out a photograph. Dawn knew it at once — Joan McInnes and her tennis partner.

"Where did you get this?"

"Mrs. Crombie," Dawn said.

"Why?"

"She showed it to me. She said I could have it." She tried to explain. "You were smiling."

Mrs. Stewart looked at the photo. Perhaps she saw the smile and it enraged her. "She had no right." She stood up violently. "I won't have people inter" — she tore the photo in two — "fering." Tore it again. Then she ran to the stove, took the poker, lifted the top, and dropped the scraps of photo in the embers. She clanged down the top.

"They ignore me for twenty years and now they inter-fere." With each syllable she banged the poker on the stove. Flames flared inside as the photo caught.

It may have been the flames, or perhaps her violence itself, that alarmed her. She looked at Dawn with fright in her eyes.

"Oh, Dawn, help me."

Dawn went to her.

"Dawn, we've got to get out of this place."

"Where to?"

"I can't stay here any longer. We've got to get away."

She went to the door and threw it open as though she meant to leave that very minute.

A car was at the gate. A man was walking up the drive.

He, poor fellow, was Mr. Simpson, dairy inspector. He was only doing his job, as he insisted later on. There was something nervous in his approach. He knew Mrs. Stewart's temper from earlier visits; and, in fact, he had gone to the police station in town to try to persuade Bob Davies to go with him to the farm. But Davies had other fish to fry.

"Just be polite," he advised Simpson. "She's only a woman."

So Simpson tried being polite.

"Ken Simpson, Mrs. Stewart. Department of Agriculture. We've met before. Lovely morning."

"What do you want?"

"Oh, just a little look in your shed. Nothing serious."

"You're supposed to give me notice before you come around here."

"Well, war time, Mrs. Stewart. You know how it is."

"No, I don't. Get off my farm."

"Now, now—"

"Don't you 'now now' me. Go on, clear out, before I set my dogs on you."

"I'm sorry, Mrs. Stewart, but I've got a job to do. We've had a complaint—"

"Complaint?"

"About your milk. I have to investigate."

"Who complained?" Mrs. Stewart came down the steps into the yard. Dawn followed her.

"Grandma."

Simpson smiled at her, trying to make things easy. "Hello, girlie." It didn't work.

"Don't you dare talk to my granddaughter." She stepped up to him, forcing him back.

"Hey!" Simpson said.

"Get off my farm. Off! Off!"

She had gone crazy, Simpson said. She looked as if she had red-hot marbles instead of eyes.

"Very well," he said, "but I'll be back. And I'll bring the police. I have a legal right to look in your shed." He went past the truck and saw the urn. He tapped it with his fingers and heard liquid inside. "Is there milk in there? Out in the sun? I'm going to take a sample of that."

Mrs. Stewart ran to his side. "Sample?" She leaped on the back of the truck. "I'll give you samples." She lifted the urn easily and swamped him with a great thick stream of milk. (Or, as Miss Betts said, water and milk.) And Dawn confessed to Grandma that if it hadn't been so horrible she would have laughed at Simpson standing there with his hair soaked down and milk dripping off his nose and chin. He slapped his chest and a fat squirt of liquid jumped like a frog from his jacket pocket.

Meanwhile — there are lots of *meanwhiles* in this part of the story — Jack was in the water again, feeling the launch hull and not liking what he found; Mom and Grandma were setting off on their gasoline-stealing expedition; Dad was in the shop taking bets and tuning the radio for the Ellerslie races, already deep in Saturday, his favorite day; I was standing by to act as runner; and Bob Davies was getting ready to fry his other fish, which was Dad.

I didn't like my Saturday job. I had to keep it secret from Mom and that made me guilty. And it seemed a shameful thing to be making money from bets when the war was on.

"Smile or your face will stay that way," Dad said.

George Perry came sliding in. "Time for a bet in the first, Alf?"

"Sure. Wait in the back." There were already half a dozen men out there playing snooker. I heard them laughing and calling friendly insults at each other, and thought of Jack alone on the launch. I kept on feeling a sinking in my stomach. How could he hope to hide for the rest of the war? Alone all the time? No one to talk to? With MPs hunting him? I wanted to go back to the launch and say I would go with him.

Dad told me half a dozen names. "Okay, Destry, ride." He saw my reluctance and pushed me toward the door. "An extra bob if you're back in ten minutes." He gave me a wink. "Eyes front when you pass the cop-shop." It was one of those times when I didn't like my father very much.

I rode up the street, turned down a side street, knocked at a door. Dad was crafty. His customers had numbers—no names were written down. So, "No. 26," I wrote on a piece of paper, "5 shillings each way on Tom Thumb. No. 33, 10 shillings place on Queen Mab"—or whatever the names were. I heard Grandma's motorcycle and saw it flash across the intersection, but thought nothing of it.

Riding back to the shop, I passed the police station. Eyes front, as I had been taught. But at the last moment I turned my head. A constable I'd never seen was standing in the door. It worried me. Were they going to search for Jack again?

I handed my list of bets to Dad. He sat throned in the revolving chair with his ledger on his knee and started transcribing. "That's a donkey," he snickered, writing the first bet.

I looked in the poolroom, watched the men. Balls clicked and sped and thumped into the pockets.

"Great shot!"

"You lucky devil."

It wasn't fair that Jack had to be alone. And these men here, smoking and playing snooker, while he had to fight in the war and maybe get killed. Just for a moment I knew that I would run away if Japanese with bayonets came through the jungle after me.

I turned to Dad. "There's a new policeman at the station."

He looked up. After his scare with the sugar Dad was more alert. A new policeman might mean danger to him. He closed his ledger, stepped out of the chair, went to the door. He put his head out and looked up the street. In front of the station Davies and the constable were getting in Davies's car. It started, made a U-turn, and headed down the street toward the shop.

I had never seen Dad move so fast. "C'm'ere." He grabbed my shirt and stuffed the ledger in. He stuffed in the sheet of bets, then darted to the wastepaper basket and grabbed pieces of paper from there. Into my shirt they went. Then he shoved me in the chair. He opened a cupboard, took a sheet, flipped it open, had it around my neck and tucked in before I was settled. Back to the cupboard. A fresh apron. Over his head, a bow at the back. Dad seized his comb and clippers. And when the car stopped and Davies and the constable—Forbes was his name—came striding in, there I was sheeted in the chair and Dad humming a tune and clipping away, cutting a neat track in my hair. A lucky thing for him it needed cutting.

He grinned at them. "Sorry, gents, shop's closed Saturdays. Just doing a free one for my boy."

Davies flashed a piece of paper at him. "I've got a warrant to search these premises." He jerked this thumb at Forbes. "In the back. No one leaves." Forbes went into the poolroom.

"Search?" Dad said. His face was hurt. "You're searching me? What are you looking for, a whiskey still?"

"Shut up, Alf." Davies snapped his fingers at me. "Skedaddle, son."

"He's not finished."

"Finish him later. Go on, buzz off."

Dad untucked the sheet. I saw his eyes go flick to make sure no paper was sticking out of my shirt.

"I'm amazed," he said to Davies.

"Sure you are."

I got out of the chair. It seemed to me the ledger in my shirt made me look as fat as Billy Bunter in the comic book. I put my hand on it and went to the door a little bent over.

"Stomach ache," I mumbled at Davies.

"Too much Yankee candy. Greedy, these kids," Dad said.

I reached my bike, wheeled it away, then jumped on and pedaled up the street, expecting Davies's voice to call me back. Then I wondered where to go. Not home. When they found nothing in the shop they might search there. So I went down a side street and got on the road to Grandma and Grandpa's place. They could look after the ledger. It was all I could think of to do.

As I turned into the river road a car went by, heading for town. The driver looked very odd, I thought. His hair was plastered on his skull as though he'd used a whole jar of Brylcreem.

At the shop Dad was having fun. He sat in the chair and watched Davies search.

"I know, it's that runaway Yank."

Davies opened a drawer.

"He's not in there."

"Shut up." An announcer started describing a horse race on the radio. Davies switched it off nastily. He finished his search.

"Right. We'll start out back. You first."

"Pleasure. But you're barking up the wrong tree, Bob."

They went into the poolroom. The players had stopped their games and were leaning on the tables watching Forbes rummage in the seats along the wall.

"There's a safe in here," he said to Davies.

Davies smiled. At last! Dad smiled too. "Watch out for wetas."

Forbes jerked back.

"Great big jaws." Dad mimed them biting, then said to the men, "Carry on, gents, we're just spring cleaning."

"Key, Alf," Davies said in a gritty voice.

Dad fished it out of his watch pocket and handed it over. Davies, taking his time, prolonging his anticipation, opened the safe. The only thing inside was a prewar racing form, a souvenir of one of Dad's big wins. Davies snatched it up and riffled through the pages. "What else do you keep in here? What's usually here?"

"Bars of gold. The family jewels," Dad said.

Forbes had gone to stand by the back door, blocking George, who looked as if he meant to slide away. He looked out the window.

"Hey," he said, and beckoned to Davies. "There's two women siphoning gas out there."

Davies went past the tables and looked out. He gave a nasty grin at Dad.

"You've got burglars."

Mom and Grandma were siphoning from the hearse. They looked up, unconcerned, as Davies and Dad and all the rest spilled out of the poolroom—although Mom confessed to me her heart went flip.

"What are you ladies up to?" Davies said.

"Ber! Mom!" Dad cried.

Grandma smiled at them. "I needed some gasoline—"

"—so I'm giving her some," Mom completed it. She held up her finger at Dad. "Be quiet, Alf, it's in the family." Then to Davies: "What's going on, Bob?"

"I've got a warrant to search here, Mrs. Pascoe."

"What for?" Mom frowned at Dad. "I hope Rex is not involved in this."

Dad tried to shush her. He didn't want Davies remembering me. And perhaps Davies would have worked it out, but he had no time. Footsteps sounded in the poolroom. A man came out and darted at Davies. His hair was stuck on his forehead in a shark's tooth pattern. His shoes made a squishing sound. He smelled of milk.

Davies couldn't believe it. "What happened to you?"

"You come . . . You come with me." He was so angry he could hardly speak. "There's someone I want you to arrest."

18

Jack Goes to Sea

I was riding on the long stretch of road by Stewarts' farm when I looked back and saw Davies's car turn the corner. Naturally I thought he was chasing me. I put my head down and rode as fast as I could. The ledger weighed like lead in my shirt.

I passed the farm gate and started up the hill, losing speed, and knew Davies would catch me before I reached the top. It never crossed my mind to give myself up. I thought if Dad was arrested he'd go to prison, and I couldn't stand that. So halfway up I stopped and threw my bike down at the side of the road and ran into the bracken. If I could get into the gully I had a good chance of getting away. Or maybe I could hide the ledger there and walk out whistling with an empty shirt. But as I climbed the fence into the farm, I heard the car stop. I perched on the top wire, looking back, and saw Davies and Simpson get out of the car.

Davies had seen me all right, seen me run, and he had put two and two together.

"You stay where you are, boy," he yelled. "If you're not on top of that fence when I come back I'll wring your neck."

He and Simpson walked up the drive. When they went from sight I hopped off the fence. Plenty of time to hide the ledger and get back on top before he came. I ran down to the gully and found a bracken patch and hid the book down among the dry roots, with all the scraps of paper stuffed inside. Then I grew curious about what might be happening on the farm. Why was Davies going there? Maybe it had something to do with Jack. So I slid down through the ferns and jumped the little creek and crept up the other side of the gully where I found a place with a clear view of the house.

Davies and Simpson were crossing the yard.

As they approached, Mrs. Stewart opened the door. She stood looking down at the men.

Davies went straight to the point. "Did you do that, Mrs. Stewart?" — indicating Simpson, who was drying out in the sun and starting to steam.

"He looked as if he could do with a wash," she tried to joke. It made Simpson furious.

"You're mad. I've filed a complaint. You're getting arrested."

"Complaints, is it?" Her composure broke. She started shaking. "My husband went away and got gassed and died. . . . I worked this farm for twenty years without any help. . . . I raised this girl . . ." (Dawn, in the kitchen, behind her.)

"Mrs. Stewart," Davies said, in a softer tone, though still firmly. She took no notice.

"And he comes here and talks about complaints . . ."

"You can't dump milk on him, Mrs. Stewart."

"I was putting him off my farm. You go too. Go on, get out."

"I think you'd better come back to town with me."

"Arresting me?" She could not believe it.

"No," Davies said easily.

"What about my complaints? People come and try to poison my dogs. They come out here and shout things at me—"

"Come on, Mrs. Stewart."

"No!"

She reached down beside the door and brought out a shotgun. As Davies stepped at her she leveled it.

"I'm not going into Kettle Creek. Get off my land."

Simpson backed off. He started to run. Davies stood his ground.

"Hey now, Mrs. Stewart, give me that. You'll hurt someone."

"I'll shoot you. I'll shoot anyone."

Davies saw Dawn's scared face behind her.

"Dawn," he said, "you go out the back door and go down to the road and wait in my car."

"Stay there, Dawn," Mrs. Stewart shouted.

"Let me take the girl. Then we can talk."

"No one's taking Dawn. She's mine."

"Come on," Davies said soothingly. He took a step toward her. She cocked the gun and raised it and aimed at his chest.

"I'm going to shoot."

He knew that if he took another step, she'd pull the trigger.

"No, I'm going." He took several slow steps back. "You put that gun away. I'll come back soon with some of your friends, then we can talk."

"I'll shoot anyone who comes past my gate."

"We'll see. Now you and Dawn go inside and have a cup of tea. And take it easy, eh? Everything's all right." So he retreated, and turned his back, and walked away steadily down the drive.

Simpson was waiting at the car. Davies gave him the keys. "Get Constable Forbes out here. I'll stay and watch the girl."

"Right," Simpson said. He was happy to get away.

"Tell him to bring Mrs. Crombie."

Simpson drove away, and Davies looked back at the house. The door was closed. He risked going halfway back up the drive. It was a mistake.

The door opened and Mrs. Stewart came out. She

had left her gun inside and Davies saw his chance. He started running up the drive. From my place in the trees I saw what she was doing and I opened my mouth to yell a warning. Too late. I made no sound. The dogs were free.

"Sic him, Dave! Sic him, Dot! Go on! Get him!"

They came around the shed into Davies's view, sighted him and ran at him like greyhounds from a starting gate, with that hideous yammering-yelping blood-hungry sound some hunting dogs make.

Davies might have tried to calm one dog or fight it off. No chance with two. He looked around, saw only one tree close, vaulted the fence, ran for it. The dogs lost speed scrambling through the wires. He reached the tree, a manuka, leaped into it, whipped his ankles almost out of their jaws, and sat there swaying in the skinny tree, only six inches clear of Dave and Dot's leaping.

In the kitchen Mrs. Stewart grabbed a sack from under the bench. She gave it to Dawn.

"Hold it. Open it, girl."

She flung wide cupboard doors and threw food in the sack, whatever was there. The shotgun was lying on the table.

"Where are we going?" Dawn said. She was terrified. While her grandmother was letting the dogs go, she had tried to take the cartridges from the gun but hadn't been able to get it open.

Mrs. Stewart fixed her eyes on her. "They'll take you

away. They'll lock me up. You don't want to go away from
me, Dawn?"

"No," Dawn said.

"I've been your mother."

"Yes."

Mrs. Stewart smiled, a crazy cunning in her eyes.

"I know a place we can hide."

I saw them coming out the back door. Mrs. Stewart had
her gun. Dawn carried the sack on her shoulder. They
went fifty yards before Davies spotted them.

"Mrs. Stewart!" he yelled.

"Stay, Dave. Stay, Dot. Sic him."

He tried kicking the dogs but one caught the cuff of his
trousers and he had to tear it free. The tree swayed. If he
didn't keep it balanced it would bend over gracefully and
serve him to the dogs like a lamb roast.

I hoped he would be safe. There was nothing I could do.
I ran down the gully and up the other side to see if Mrs.
Stewart and Dawn were heading where I thought.

They were. I saw Dawn stop and Mrs. Stewart push
her on.

No, I wanted to yell, don't go there, Dawn. But I knew
there was no way she could stop her grandma. They
reached the path into the mangroves. Mrs. Stewart took
the sack and made Dawn climb the fence. She handed the
sack over and climbed herself.

I turned and ran. Up the paddock. Along the road. Leo
was thinning grapes with pruning shears.

"Leo!"

He looked up.

"Mrs. Stewart's making Dawn go on the launch. She's got a gun."

Jack heard the wires squeak. When there was no signal he thought it must be Mom and Grandma coming back. Then he heard Mrs. Stewart's voice.

"Careful with that sack. You're going to drop it."

There was no time to get in the canoe. He slipped into the deckhouse and watched. In a moment Dawn climbed onto the dock and Mrs. Stewart scrambled up behind.

"Wait," Mrs. Stewart said. She looked suspiciously at the launch. "Someone's been here."

"Only me," Dawn said. "I use it." She hoped that Jack had got away. Then she saw the nose of the canoe beyond the launch and knew he must be hiding in the deckhouse.

"Let's go somewhere else, Grandma. This is no good."

"Someone's been here." She saw the movement of Jack's head as he looked out. She cocked the gun.

"You. Whoever you are. Come out."

So Jack stepped out of the deckhouse and smiled at her. "Howdy, ma'am. I hope you don't mind me using your launch."

"Hands up. Don't move." She made her way along the dock and climbed onto the launch, her gun never wavering from its aim. Dawn came behind her.

"Jack's been hiding here. We've been helping him. It's my fault."

"Back inside," Mrs. Stewart said. He went into the deckhouse. She followed and looked around. She took in the quilt, the cupboards, the photograph of Rose. "Do you know my daughter?" Odd things were happening in her mind. Perhaps she thought Jack was Jimmy, Dawn's father.

Jack's eyes were on the gun. "No, lady, I've never met her."

She took the bottle of perfume from her pocket. "Did you give my granddaughter this?"

"I'm scared of guns. Put it down."

"Did you?" A shout.

"My mother gave it to me," Dawn cried. She saw Jack move. "Don't, it's loaded. Grandma, all he's been doing is trying to make the launch go."

Mrs. Stewart nodded. She seemed to work out something in her mind. "All right. Make it go now," she said.

We heard the engine cough as we ran down the paddock. It sounded like a sick cow. Then it gave several weak little putters — and it caught. It gave a roar.

We reached the dock in time to see the launch turning out of sight around the mangroves, with the canoe bumping at its side. Jack was in the wheelhouse and Dawn was in there too. Mrs. Stewart was on the rear deck, holding her gun. She saw us and swung it around. We ran back along the dock.

"On the cliff," I cried.

We ran across the slope of the hill and reached the low

cliff above the river. The launch came nosing out of the creek and turned toward the sea.

"Where are they going?"

"They can't get out," Leo said. "They'll get stuck on the bar."

The launch came along below us. Mrs. Stewart had her gun pointing at the wheelhouse. Then Dawn came out. "She's making Dawn untie the canoe."

"Jack will lose all his stuff."

"Untie it. Do what I say," shouted Mrs. Stewart.

"Grandma—"

"Do it Dawn," Jack said from the wheel.

So Dawn untied the canoe and left it bobbing in the wake. The launch chugged on, so slow a swimmer could have kept up with it. Jack listened to the sound of the engine.

"I don't like the sound of her, ma'am."

"Keep on going."

"Can't get over that bar. Too many waves."

"We're leaking," Dawn cried.

"Yeah, thought she might. She's opening up with the vibration," Jack said. "Have to head for shore."

"No! The other side, go over there."

"We'll never make it."

"You go where I tell you." She threatened him with the gun.

"Whatever you say." Jack was waiting his chance. He took the old lifejacket from its nail and threw it to Dawn. "Put that on."

She looked at her grandma. Mrs. Stewart nodded. Dawn put the lifejacket on while the launch turned slowly and headed out across the estuary. She saw Leo and me on the cliff.

"We're sinking," she screamed.

Just like Mom and Grandma, we had the same idea at the same time. We ran across the hill—I can still feel those grass heads whipping my shins—and came to Grandma and Grandpa's house. The shed was open and the amphibian sat inside—unnatural, boat on wheels, crazy machine. We jumped in. The keys were in the ignition. I remembered my lessons in driving it—Jack's voice, "Easy with your foot on that clutch." Out of the shed we chugged, across the yard, down the paddock, moving like a flat four-legged beetle in the grass.

Grandpa ran out of the house.

"Rex!" I heard him yell.

"We'll bring it back soon, Grandpa."

"Rex . . ." His voice was lost in the engine noise. What he was saying, I found out later, was that he'd run out of tar and all the leaks were not fixed yet.

Leo ran ahead, opening gates. I drove down the track to the beach where we had launched the canoe. Leo came jumping on board. Over the mud and sand we went, into the water, and for a moment we thought the wheels would refuse to leave the bottom and we'd end up driving on the riverbed. At last though we felt some buoyancy, the boat floated, and I changed the engine over—which was difficult; I'd only seen Grandpa demonstrate in the shed—

changed it to drive the propeller shaft. It started to turn
with a deafening clatter in its metal bed and the boat felt as
if a weak hand were pushing it. We looked at each other,
appalled. We could walk heel to toe faster than this. The
launch was halfway over the estuary. We'd never catch it.

Jack looked at the water on the deck. It was coming up so
fast you could see it rise.

"Guess ole *Rose* wasn't meant to go."

"No," Dawn whispered.

"We're not going to make it, lady. Best turn back," he
told Mrs. Stewart.

"We'll turn back when I say. Can't we go faster?"

"Listen to that motor. Lucky she's going at all. Hey,
that gun'll go off the way you're squeezin'."

"It'll go off when I want it to. Dawn, find something to
bail with."

"Bucket's up front," Jack said, "but it won't do no
good." Then he saw his chance as Mrs. Stewart turned. He
reached her in two steps, grabbed the barrel of the gun,
forced it down and around, away from Dawn. One barrel
went off and blasted a hole the size of a soup plate in the
hull. Jack wrestled it away and threw it over the engine
cowling. Mrs. Stewart fought to get to it. He put his arms
around her and lifted her up. Dawn thought he was going
to throw her overboard.

"Don't," she screamed. But Jack was simply trying to
keep her still. They fell and lay tangled in the door of the

deckhouse. At that moment the engine stopped. In the silence Jack said, "I hope I didn't hurt you, ma'am."

Mrs. Stewart fought.

"No, you can't get up. Dawn, get the gun. Easy, now. Keep it pointed away, one barrel still loaded."

Dawn picked it up.

"Over the side."

She put it in the water and let it go. The gun sank. Jack released Mrs. Stewart. She scrambled to her feet, looked wildly round. Jack went into the deckhouse and tried to start the engine. It wouldn't go.

"Finished," he said. He gave a half-frightened look at Dawn. Tried to joke, "This ain't a good place to have a puncture."

"We've got to bail," Mrs. Stewart cried. "Where's the bucket?" She ran into the bow.

The water was up to Jack's ankles. It flowed in a little waterfall through the hole the gun had blasted.

"We're going to sink," Dawn whispered.

"You'll have to swim."

"It's too far."

"No it's not. Like you taught me." He smiled. "Like an eel."

"What about you and Grandma?"

"We'll be all right. Might last out till they send a boat."

Mrs. Stewart came back with the bucket. She started throwing water over the side. "Get the motor going," she shouted at Jack.

"Motor's finished." He gave Dawn a little push. "Move, girl."

"Grandma?" Dawn said.

But Mrs. Stewart kept working with her bucket, splashing water over the side.

"Go on," Jack said.

Dawn put her leg over the side. She lowered herself, but held on and did not want to let go.

"Swim hard," Jack said. He freed her hands and pushed her away.

The amphibian was leaking too. We knew we would never reach the launch.

"Bail with your hands," I cried.

"We'll have to turn back."

Far away, the launch was very low. The deckhouse looked like a little shed standing on the water.

"There's someone swimming."

We saw a flash of paddling hands, a head sleek as wet stone.

"It's Dawn."

"Dawn! This way! Over here!"

She turned feebly. She was very weak.

"Slow down," Leo yelled at me. But the amphibian had one speed and all I could do was aim at Dawn and slide by. Leo grabbed at her and missed. I turned the amphibian, a slow, heavy, ugly, laboring turn. We came at Dawn again. Leo managed to get hold of the lifejacket. She could not turn to lock her hands on his.

"I can't get her."

I saw my BB gun lying in the bilges. I left the tiller, grabbed the gun, held it barrel first at Dawn. She reached it with one hand—and that way, as the amphibian spun around like a bee on the water, we managed to turn her toward us, and get four hands on her, and pull her on board.

When we looked again, the launch was gone.

We sank too, thirty yards from shore. But Matty and Gloria had swum for the canoe and they paddled up as we went down. They pulled Dawn into the cockpit and Leo and I held on to the sides and we made it to the beach—where, it seemed, the whole town was waiting.

Stipan plowed in, grabbed Leo and me, put one of us under each arm. Davies—someone had rescued him from the dogs—grabbed Dawn from the canoe and carried her in and gave her to Grandma. Mom and Dad were there, Grandpa was there—dozens of people. We stood in a group and stared out over the estuary, where several boats were moving toward the place where the launch had been. We watched them circle, blindly searching.

Dawn's map, my *Champion,* a half-empty bottle—that is the sort of thing they found. And two days later searchers found Mrs. Stewart's body on the bar. They never found Jack.

Dawn stayed with Grandma Crombie for a week. Then her mother came and took her away and I never heard what

Blairsville High School Library

happened after that. I like to think she was happy with her mother. Leo and I stayed friends for the rest of the year. Then we went to schools in town, mine the public school and his a Roman Catholic one, and made different friends and did not see so much of each other. He still lives in Kettle Creek and runs the vineyard with Matty—who married someone else, not Gloria. They make good wine and win lots of medals.

I study insects at the Department of Scientific and Industrial Research. I'm writing a book about wetas. And, of course, I've written one about Jack. Here it is. I had to write it. As I said at the beginning, he's the most important person I've ever known.

I often wonder what happened on the launch at the very end. Jack probably tried to save Mrs. Stewart. That is the sort of thing he'd do. And then perhaps he tried to swim ashore. He could dog-paddle, after all. He wouldn't give up. And sometimes I wonder if he made it—just kept on kicking, paddling, as we'd taught him. Reached the other shore and pulled himself through the mangroves there. Was that someone moving, someone slipping quietly away? And he hid in the bush, up the coast where Dawn had shown him on her map, and somehow managed to survive—rabbit stoo—and traveled to Chicago after the war. He's in Chicago now, living happily. . . .

It's a dream. Perhaps I don't need to dream it anymore. I've never forgotten Jack, and never will.

About the Author

Maurice Gee is one of the most distinguished writers for children and adults in New Zealand. *The Champion* is his second book for children to be published in the United States. It is based on Mr. Gee's memories of his childhood during the Second World War. "I remember vividly the arrival of the U.S. soldiers in my home town," he says. "They came out in their jeeps (we had never seen jeeps) to buy wine from the vineyards, and we made friends with them. I wrote *The Champion* from my own experience, but invented Jack and his life on the launch."

Mr. Gee also wrote the screenplay for the television miniseries based on *The Champion*. He lives with his wife in Wellington, New Zealand.